CHRISTMAS REVELATIONS

Reluctant 1920s debutante Annabel prefers horses to suitors. When she tumbles into the path of Lawrence, Lord Lassiter, she's annoyed that this attractive man is the despised thirteenth guest joining her family for Christmas — for he has been involved in a recent scandal, and only he and his faithful valet, Norman Bassett, know the truth behind the gossip. Meanwhile, as Lawrence tries to charm Annabel, Norman has a surprise encounter with a figure from his past — one who has been keeping a secret from him for years . . .

JILL BARRY

CHRISTMAS REVELATIONS

Complete and Unabridged

LINFORD
Leicester

First published in Great Britain

First Linford Edition
published 2016

A catalogue record for this book is available
from the British Library.

ISBN 978–1–4448–3016–3

Published by
F. A. Thorpe (Publishing)
Anstey, Leicestershire

Set by Words & Graphics Ltd.
Anstey, Leicestershire
Printed and bound in Great Britain by
T. J. International Ltd., Padstow, Cornwall

This book is printed on acid-free paper

December, 1925

The sun still shone as Annabel Crawford rode her chestnut filly back into her father's stable yard. The clip-clop of Juno's hooves upon paving stones soon brought a young stable boy to meet her.

'Thank you, Tommy.' Annabel dismounted as the lad kept hold of her horse's bridle. 'Juno did well. Flew over that wall with no trouble at all.'

'I'd best keep that information under my hat, I think, miss.'

'Thank you! I know I shouldn't trespass on someone else's land, but I can do with the practice.'

The lad gave her a slow wink. 'If you say so, miss.'

'If I can't ride tomorrow, could I ask you to take Juno out, please? My mother's sure to have a hundred jobs waiting.'

'Tomorrow's Christmas Eve, after all's

said and done, miss. There must be lots to do to get ready for the festivities.'

'It'll be lovely to see all the family, but sometimes I wish something exciting would happen, Tommy.'

'Ain't Christmas exciting enough for you, miss? Lots of people around, and your Boxing Day party.'

'Tommy, if it's a choice between talking about horses with you and the others, or dancing with boring young men, you know which I'd prefer!'

'If you can manage to slip away for a ride tomorrow, it'd be good. Harold's got the day off for his sister's wedding.'

'Well that's exciting for him, but you'll be one man short in the stables.'

'Don't you worry, Miss Annabel, we'll cope all right, you see if we don't.'

'No, Tommy. You've given me the perfect excuse. I'd much rather muck out than join in drawing-room silliness.' She called over her shoulder as she headed for the house, 'Tomorrow it is, then.'

★ ★ ★

Lily Crawford looked up as her daughter entered her sitting room. 'Annabel, thank goodness you're back safe and sound.'

'I've been putting Juno through her paces, Ma, not climbing Mount Everest. I can't be late if Pa's not here yet.'

Mrs Crawford picked up her sherry glass. 'No, dear. It's just you and me today.'

'He's lying low at the office, I imagine.' Annabel's lips twitched.

'He telephoned with very exciting news.'

'Let me guess. Amelia Earhart plans to land her aeroplane in the top field and spend Christmas with us!'

'Better than that, I fancy.'

Annabel opened her mouth to protest.

'Your father has invited the Viscount Lassiter for Christmas.'

'Never heard of the old buffer. How do you and Pa know him, anyway?'

'We don't. One of your father's racing friends has begged a favour on behalf of his lordship. The Viscount Lassiter and his fiancée were planning to spend the holiday on his family's estate near Bath, but circumstances have changed.'

'How?'

Mrs Crawford leaned forward. 'Lawrence, Lord Lassiter, has broken off his engagement, that's why. Socially, it's a disaster. He has plenty of friends in Somerset and London, but the poor young man's anxious not to wash his dirty linen in public.'

'I'll bet he is.'

'As you can imagine, his mother's heartbroken. His father's advice is for him to keep out of everyone's way. Your father says no one could blame Lawrence for wanting to keep a low profile.'

'Well, I for one can blame him very easily indeed. Especially as, if my arithmetic's correct, that'll make thirteen of us at table.'

'But Annabel, imagine all those wagging tongues! Think of the embarrassment. His lordship will be much better off keeping a low profile here in Wiltshire.'

'I still think it's a rotten trick to play

on an unsuspecting girl, so close to Christmas. Why doesn't the silly man take a room in a hotel instead of gate-crashing a party of respectable people who are strangers to him anyway?'

Her mother coughed delicately. 'All we know is that his lordship's a charming young man, with the advantage of being one of the most eligible bachelors in England.'

'So what?'

'I sometimes wonder why your father spent all that money on finishing school fees.'

Annabel felt her heart bump in dismay. She might have known there'd be more to her mother's agreement to this intrusion than a mere example of good will at this festive time.

The ornate gold clock on the mantel chimed the hour. Mrs Crawford rose. 'Luncheon. Afterwards we'll make a few changes. His lordship must have the largest guest bedroom, which means Celia and Freddie can go in the white room this year.'

'Even though there are two of them and only one viscount?'

'We must afford his lordship the best possible hospitality. Surely you realise what a chance this is?'

Annabel's worst fear was out of the cage and sneering. 'Don't talk such piffle, Ma!'

'Please don't speak to me like that, Annabel.'

'All right, I apologise. But I want you to know matchmaking isn't an option. You may consider this man a good catch, but don't expect me to flutter my eyelashes. Nobleman or not, your thirteenth person at table sounds like an utter cad — and if you place me beside him for Christmas dinner, I'll jolly well take my meal outside and eat it with the horses.'

'All right, darling.'

Annabel glared in vain. Lily Crawford's thoughts were already elsewhere. 'You might ask Violet to make up the spare bed in the footman's room,' she said. 'I can't have you roaming the servants' quarters.'

'I might have known this man would bring his own staff. What a fuss.'

'It's to be expected that his valet should travel with him. The man will assist our staff and that can only be an asset. Jeffers will be in total charge, of course.'

★ ★ ★

Mrs Petts ruled her culinary domain with help from her daughter Emmie plus Violet, who walked from the village each morning. The annual festive house party required extra pairs of hands, though Mrs Petts had been known to insist she was better off with those used to working with her. While the cook, white apron tied tightly around her neat figure, slid fillets of sole on a silver serving dish, Violet sprinkled chopped parsley over boiled potatoes and carrots.

'Good job his lordship's bringing a valet,' said Mrs Petts. 'What with the footman cutting greenery and Mr

Jeffers putting up the decorations, you'll have to serve luncheon today. It's only the two ladies.'

'Will the viscount's man be working with us then? Won't he think himself above that?'

'I'm told Lord Lassiter's valet will assist wherever Mr Jeffers needs him. His lordship's expected tomorrow, in time for afternoon tea. Don't let me forget to put that tray of shortbread in the oven later.'

'Maybe the valet will be really handsome. Oops!' Violet knocked a carrot on the floor.

'Watch what you're about, my girl! No, don't put it back in the dish.' The cook sighed. 'What will I do with you?'

'Sorry, Mrs P.'

Mrs Petts shook her head. 'Don't mind me. With so much to do, we all need to work together. You can take that food in now, Violet, there's a good girl. The lemon mousse is on the sideboard and Madam says they'll serve themselves.'

The cook watched Violet load the tray and went ahead to open the door for her before turning her attention elsewhere.

'How are you doing with those marzipan fruits, Emmie?'

Her daughter looked up. 'What do you think?'

The cook peered at the latest batch — strawberries frosted with caster sugar, leaves formed from green marzipan. 'I think you've missed your vocation, my girl. You should be training as a pastry cook.' She shot a thoughtful look at Emmie.

'I'm really enjoying this. Desserts are my favourite thing of all.'

'That's a good job, seeing as you'll be whipping egg whites for the meringues after lunch.'

She turned round as Violet returned, then addressed them both, hands on hips. 'Now listen to me, you two. The next few days will be hell on wheels. You're both good girls, but you'll need all your wits about you, so no skiving off to visit the stable lads. And no making eyes at his lordship's valet!'

The two girls giggled.

'I don't care whether he looks like Rudolph Valentino or the back of a bus. It'd be a relief to find he's old enough to be your father.'

'You haven't mentioned Mr George.' Emmie nodded at Violet. 'I've already warned Vi about wandering hands. He hasn't been back home since she joined us.'

Mrs Petts' eyebrows shot up. 'I should hope that young man's corners have been rubbed off since working in London. His elder brother was never a nuisance like George.'

'Mr George is handsome though. Those dark eyes and thick eyelashes!'

Violet smothered a giggle as she caught sight of the cook's expression.

'You keep your eyes on your work, my girl. Anything more than that can only spell disaster. As for you, Violet, I thought you were walking out with the blacksmith's lad?'

10

Violet's winter pale cheeks suddenly rivalled the strawberry sweetmeats. 'He hasn't long asked. Anyway, no harm in a girl looking, is there?'

'There is, if it's Mr George Crawford Junior she's looking at. You could do far worse than the blacksmith's son. George Junior spells trouble, you mark my words.'

'He'd never look at someone like me. Even I'm not daft enough to think that's on the cards.'

The cook shook her head. 'You've a pretty face. That's all I'm saying. Don't go letting him talk you into riding in that car of his.'

'As if he'd do that. He must know there'll be girls all over him at the Boxing Night party.'

Mrs Petts sighed. 'Remember what I always say to Emmie — there's girls that will and there's girls that won't. And that holds good, whether they're born with a silver spoon in their mouths or not.'

'Which is best, d'you reckon?'

'You mean wealth or class? All I know

is they don't always go hand in hand.' Mrs Petts lowered her voice. 'I shouldn't be talking like this, but you two know better than to gossip.'

''Course we do,' said Emmie.

'This family are rolling in money. But they're what Mr Jeffers calls 'noovoh rich'. They mix with the nobs and entertain them like there's no tomorrow. But that young lord that's coming to stay, he'd better hold on to his pedigree, if you ask me.'

'Why? I don't get it.'

Emmie looked pityingly at Violet. 'Mum means Mr and Mrs Crawford will be looking to Miss Annabel to marry into the upper class and raise their standing. Isn't that right, Mum?'

The cook nodded. 'It could be an interesting few days. Now, Vi, you can call Mr Jeffers for his lunch, but don't you go letting on what we've been talking about. If you do, I'll have your guts for garters and that's a promise.'

* * *

'I thought we'd stop for a spot of lunch in Devizes, Bassett.'

'Very good, my lord.'

'You can take the wheel afterwards. I know you can't wait to get your hands on this old girl.'

Lawrence enjoyed driving his gleaming red Bentley. But Bassett, who'd been his valet since his lordship came down from Oxford and took a position in his uncle's London law firm, also drove with skill.

'It will be my pleasure, sir. I took the liberty of checking the mileage from Devizes to Starminster and if my calculations are correct, it's a little under twenty.'

'Good show.' Lawrence bit his lip. 'We should reach the manor house well in time for tea. Except I can't say I'm looking forward to this house party, you know. Not one little bit. Mind you, it's good of George Crawford to take us in. It was out of the question for me to remain at home, given my mother's reaction to what's happened, but I jolly well wish we could have stayed put.'

'Understandable to feel like that, sir, if I may say so.'

'Of course you may, Bassett. I don't know how I'd have coped these last few days without you taking most of the flak.'

'All part of the job, sir. At least no one will know your whereabouts.'

'Absolutely. And what a relief that is. Claridges is a tiptop hotel, but I couldn't believe how many folk recognised me during our stay. The only respite I got was when you lent me an outfit and I sneaked out for a breath of air. I've never been so delighted to see Hyde Park.'

'I'm pleased to have been of assistance. With respect to the gentlemen of the press, they can be a confounded nuisance at times.'

Lawrence heaved a sigh. 'I really can't think why I've suddenly become so interesting. A broken engagement is hardly the stuff of high drama, is it? It's not something of national importance.'

'With respect, you have a certain social standing, my lord. And your, er, former fiancée does have that royal connection.'

'I suppose so. Lucinda gets on very well with her cousin twice removed, or whatever it is, and reporters can't get enough of the Prince of Wales and his set.'

'I'd venture to say it's all the more important that you escape the limelight and hope some other news captures everyone's attention.'

'I don't miss her, you know, Bassett. Lucinda, I mean. I think it's probably all for the best, putting a stop to things, don't you? For the life of me I can't understand how I ever became involved with such a flibbertigibbet!'

Bassett cleared his throat. 'We're approaching the town outskirts now, sir. Would you be thinking of stopping at the Bear Hotel for luncheon?'

'Definitely. Back in my schooldays, my godfather took me there. On the way, I remember him pointing out a white horse cut from the chalky hill-side.'

'It sounds fascinating, my lord.'

'Indeed. I was only thirteen at the time but I recall the hotel's food was excellent. The Bear's an old coaching inn and with any luck there'll be a roaring log fire.' He glanced at his valet. 'You'll take your lunch with me in the dining room, of course.'

'There's no need, sir, thank you all the same. I can eat elsewhere.'

'Nonsense, Bassett. While we're in limbo, so to speak, you're my companion, and that's an end to it.'

'Whatever you wish, sir. I trust my apparel will be appropriate.'

'I doubt anyone could distinguish which of us was the valet and which the viscount. To be honest, I get more sense out of you than I do from most of the fellows I mix with.'

'I don't believe that for one minute, my lord.'

'While we eat, you can clue me in about the Crawford household. All I know is, apart from being worth a fortune, George is well-known in the racing world. There's a local hunt, according to my father, but whether they'll rustle up a mount for me on Boxing Day is another matter.'

★   ★   ★

Annabel stroked Juno's mane as the filly trotted on. She'd stood by while her mother fussed over an already immaculate guest bedroom and decided to slip away on the pretext of purchasing postage stamps. The stamps would be useful for sending thank-you letters, but also provided an excuse for Juno to gain a little more experience of the open road, with the possibility of meeting mechanical monsters on four wheels rather than four legs.

Annabel was within sight of the wrought-iron gates of the manor house, when a bird plummeted from above and landed upon Juno's shapely head. She gasped, watched the dead creature topple to the ground, and tried to calm the jittery filly. 'It's all right, Juno! The poor thing can't hurt you now.'

But the hasty response, intended to soothe, couldn't prevent the filly from rearing. She caught Annabel unawares, casting her aside like an unwanted bonnet.

Juno whinnied. Stomped around a bit. Trotted a few yards back along the road and came to a standstill. She was turning her head, swishing her mane, as if unsure what to do next, when a red Bentley rounded the bend.

'Good Lord, what's going on here?' In the passenger seat, his lordship shaded his eyes against the last rays of December afternoon sunshine. 'Hell's bells, looks like the rider's been thrown.'

'I'll pull over, sir.'

'Good job, Bassett. Leave the horse to me while you check on the rider — but whatever you do, don't mention my name. In fact, better not call me anything at all.'

The older man halted the vehicle, and Lawrence, discarding the woollen rug he'd tucked around his legs, opened his door and climbed over the running board. The beautiful filly eyed him as he moved but held her ground. In fact, he could have sworn she batted her gigantic eyelashes at him.

'There there, girl. Nothing to fear.'

He murmured more soothing words and, once close enough, raised his hand to her nostrils. She didn't move. Heartened, Lawrence gave her nose a rub. She whickered softly.

'Good girl.' He removed his hand and stepped backwards. A swift glance revealed Bassett crouched over a motionless figure at the roadside. The filly took a step towards Lawrence. 'What a good girl.' He moved his left hand slowly back to her nose, his other hand reaching for her reins. He wondered if she'd rear this time, but she still eyed him and remained placid.

He led her slowly along the highway towards Bassett and the person now sitting upright on the grass verge. Bassett appeared to be examining the person's left foot. A discarded riding boot lay beside someone who Lawrence now realised was an extremely attractive young lady.

But hadn't Lucinda beguiled him with her violet eyes and corn-silk hair? He'd been bemused by her kittenish looks, her feminine wiles and honeyed tones, not to mention her glamorous royal relations. What a fool he'd been. She'd betrayed him while he was out of town on business. By chance, she and her lover had selected for their tryst a secluded hotel where a friend of his had been dining.

Lawrence chose to bear the blame for ending their relationship. He'd done the gentlemanly thing, but only close friends knew the truth and understood his relief at avoiding marriage to someone so careless with her affections. But he knew he must curb further dangerous romantic thoughts, especially involving an unknown raven-haired beauty with melting brown eyes and a creamy complexion. Society saw him as a cad, and his offer to save

Lucinda's face had placed him in a position where he daren't look at women in any other way but as fellow human beings.

'Good afternoon. I trust you're not badly hurt. You'll be pleased to hear your horse appears unharmed.'

'The young lady's probably sprained her ankle.' Bassett looked up. 'I've suggested we give her a lift to her home.'

'Of course we must. How far away do you live, Miss, er — '

'My name's Crawford. Miss Annabel Crawford. I live at Starminster Manor, just up the road there. Do you see the gateway?'

Lawrence gulped. He cast his valet what he knew must be a desperate glance. 'With your permission, Miss Crawford, I shall lead your horse home while Mr Bassett drives you to your door.'

'That's so very civil of you. What amazing luck the two of you came along when you did.' Her low, beautifully modulated voice and radiant smile would have brightened even the gloomiest day. 'I'll direct you to the stables so one of the lads can take care of Juno.' She paused. 'Do you gentlemen live around here? I don't recall meeting either of you before.' She looked from one to the other. 'Perhaps we could offer some refreshment before you continue your journey?'

His lordship and Bassett exchanged glances. Neither spoke, until Lawrence realised how rude they must seem and how futile it would be to continue his pathetic ploy of anonymity. They could hardly accompany Miss Crawford back to the house where they were invited to spend Christmas without confessing their reason for being in the vicinity.

'I, erm, I'd like to introduce myself as Lawrence Lassiter. This is Norman Bassett.' He held out his hand. 'I imagine you know that we're to be, erm, guests of your parents.'

Annabel extended her hand. Very slowly. And, he realised with a pang, with much reluctance.

'You mean you're the viscount who's — '

Lawrence nodded. 'Fortunate enough

to be joining your house party, Miss Crawford.'

She turned towards Bassett. 'Perhaps you'd be kind enough to help me to my feet, Mr Bassett?'

Juno snorted. Lawrence glared at her. Did horses possess a sense of humour? This one seemed to enjoy his discomfiture.

'Perhaps I should bring the car closer, Miss Crawford? I'm sure his lordship's better able to deal with equine matters than I am.'

'You're very kind, Mr Bassett.'

'Top idea,' said Lawrence. 'I'll wait here with Miss Crawford and Juno.'

Annabel watched the valet sprint back to the Bentley. 'What a thoroughly nice chap he is.' But her warm tone soon chilled. 'Maybe I should try riding back. These jodhpurs are soggy and I'd hate to cause any damage to your car's upholstery, Lord Lassiter.'

'I couldn't care two hoots about a bit of damp, but shouldn't you have your ankle examined before getting back into the saddle, Miss Crawford? For starters, I don't think that swelling will allow you to wear your riding boot.'

'How annoying! If I have to sit around with my feet up, I'll be at the mercy of anyone looking to bore me with tedious tales of the play they saw last week. As for atrocities like whist and bridge, if I see anyone even opening a pack of playing cards, I'll pretend I'm asleep. I should warn you, the Vicar in particular is a demon!'

Annabel looked up at Lawrence. He couldn't prevent his lips from twitching. He knew she saw merriment sparkle in his eyes. For a moment she appeared distracted, while he fantasised about scooping her up in his arms and carrying her off, swollen foot and all, in his motorcar. Somewhere far away from other people. This image so tantalised him that he couldn't look away. Nor could she. Until, perhaps recalling she was in the company of currently the most despised member of the British aristocracy, she averted her eyes and heaved a sigh.

'This really is most inconsiderate, Annabel.'

Annabel's glare should have turned her mother to ice. 'I didn't exactly plan to fall off my horse.'

'I meant inconsiderate to sneak off for a ride instead of changing into a pretty tea gown and playing the pianoforte for Aunt Hester. You know how she loves Christmas carols.'

'How was I to know she'd arrive so early?'

'Friends were kind enough to drop her off on their way to Bath. Worst of all is how close you came to causing a bad accident. Both you and his lordship might have been injured, as well as his man.'

Annabel counted to ten. 'Where is the viscount, anyway?'

'Aunt Hester's keeping him company.'

Annabel giggled. 'Divine retribution! She's probably telling him tales of her

25

trip to the Pyramids at the turn of the century.'

'I really should join them. I can't have Lord Lassiter thinking I'm a bad hostess. It would be much easier if your father came home to help, now you're laid up.'

'I'm sure Pa won't be long. Anyway, I don't need you to stand guard over me, Mother. Someone can show the doctor where I am when he arrives.'

'This isn't the best of starts to our Christmas.' Mrs Crawford walked over to the door. 'But I'm sorry if you're in pain, my dear.'

Annabel turned her head to hide a tear. Her mother would ensure the household was well fed and entertained. But she was right; a sprained ankle was highly inconvenient. She'd planned to visit the stables early next morning and muck out Juno's box. She had gifts from Juno to hand the lads. It was so unfair!

She reached for her handkerchief as someone tapped on the sitting-room door. 'Come in.'

To her surprise, Mr Bassett stood on the threshold. 'Excuse me, Miss Annabel, but his lordship wishes to enquire after your health.'

She waved him in. 'I'm not at death's door, so do come and talk to me, Norman. You don't mind if I call you Norman?'

She watched him blink hard. 'It's a little unusual, Miss Annabel, under the circumstances.'

'Rubbish! You've carried me in your arms, placed a blanket beneath my soggy jodhpurs and driven me home after my mishap, so why stand on ceremony?'

He moved closer. 'His lordship and I were pleased to help.'

'It was rather a shock, discovering who he was.'

Bassett nodded. 'I do believe the feeling was mutual.'

'Well, you may thank Lord Lassiter for his interest. I'm still awaiting a visit from the family doctor and until he informs me what I may or may not do, I might just as well be shipwrecked.'

'If I may make so bold, Miss Annabel, if you have anything with which I might help, I shall of course do everything in my power to assist.'

'You really are a sweet man, Norman.' She saw his surprised expression. 'I mean it, you know,' she said. 'You're not like certain people I could mention.'

'Anyone would have done the same as his lordship and me, Miss Annabel.'

'Anyway, you're very kind to offer further assistance, but the main thing bothering me is Juno. If I can't get out to visit her, let alone ride her to the Boxing Day meet, I shall be heart-broken.'

'I'm no horseman, I'm afraid. Perhaps his lordship — '

She shook her head. 'I shouldn't look on the black side, but I suspect I'll be forced to sit around for the time being. There is something I can do though. Something to repay you for your kind-ness.'

'With respect, Miss Annabel, it's not necessary. You have enough to concern you.'

She looked up at him. 'Ah, but it's occurred to me that we shouldn't expect you to share our footman's room. I understand you're just as much a friend as a valet to Lord Lassiter.'

'Please don't worry yourself on my account, Miss Annabel.'

'But I insist. I can't do it myself, but I'll ensure my mother instructs someone to strip the linen from the original bed and take it to the old nursery. The bed the nanny used to sleep in is still in the little side room, and you'll have privacy and probably a twinkle-eyed teddy bear or two for company.'

The door flew open.

'Our dear doctor is here, Annabel.'

Bassett gave a slight bow in Mrs Crawford's direction and sidled towards the door.

'Thanks for keeping me company,' called Annabel. She smiled sweetly at the family doctor. 'I do hope you'll be able to strap me up somehow. It's very important I can get around to help my poor, overworked mother.'

* * *

Norman Bassett recognised her as soon as he stepped inside the kitchen. When Mr Jeffers mentioned the cook was called Mrs Petts, the name had meant nothing. Even if he'd heard her called Phyllis, it could have been any Phyllis. But fate decreed the cook should be his Phyllis. She'd aged well. Probably better than he had, having suffered the trenches as lodgings for much of the Great War years. He'd been one of the lucky ones. So many of his generation had ended their lives in Flanders. Too many tears wept. Too much blood spilled on foreign soil.

'More tea, Mr Bassett?'

'Please.' Norman returned to the present.

'You were miles away. I had to ask you twice,' said Mr Jeffers.

'I beg your pardon. I was thinking back to old times. Other kitchens I've sat in — you know the sort of thing.'

'Indeed I do. This is one of the better households. I see no reason to look elsewhere for employment.' He leaned forward. 'The family are typical nouveau riche, of course, but they try hard to fit into the kind of society you and I are used to. He nodded towards the kitchen range. 'And they've kitted the place out well. No expense spared, as you can see.'

'Have you worked for the family long?' Norman spooned sugar into his teacup.

'Four years. Mrs Petts has been cook here much longer than that. Mr Crawford and family inherited her when they purchased the manor house.' He inclined his head towards the young maid piping whipped cream on a trifle. 'Emmie there's her daughter. She's a good girl — lucky too, having a mother who can train her up. Skilful cooks can always find a position. If she keeps her head screwed on and her hand on her halfpenny, she could move to London and get a job in a smart hotel like the Savoy or the Ritz.'

'Indeed she could, if she shows promise.' Bassett shifted his position slightly. 'How about her, um, father? Might I enquire if Mr Petts works for the family too?'

'Mrs Petts is a widow, poor soul. Her husband used to work on a local farm and I'm afraid he met a most unfortunate end. Not the most pleasant of subjects for a Christmas Eve, I'm sure you'll understand.'

'Of course. Poor lady.'

Norman glanced over his shoulder at Mrs Petts, so engrossed in her cooking. He wondered if that red-gold hair, inherited by her daughter — who'd let a tendril escape from beneath her cap — still retained any of its former glory. Phyllis had taken no notice of him; probably not even seen him sit down in the alcove. Why would she? The girl called Violet had made them a pot of tea, and Mr Jeffers thought it was point-less introducing him to the staff while they were preparing Christmas Eve supper. Would Phyllis even recognise him? Would his name spark a memory?

'Finished your tea? Come on then.' Mr Jeffers rose. 'I can introduce you when we sit down for our own supper.'

Norman followed the butler, leaving be-hind simmering saucepans and appetising odours, to walk along the dimly lit cor-ridor. Mr Jeffers pushed open the door to a very different domain. As an experi-enced gentleman's valet, Norman felt equally at home walking upon luxuri-ous carpets or treading worn linoleum, but it occurred to him he mightn't feel so relaxed later, locking gazes with his old flame.

He set off to locate Lord Lassiter.

* * *

'Did she really say that thing about death's door? What a little minx the girl is.' Lawrence peered at his reflection in the cheval mirror.

'If I might say so, my lord, Miss Annabel has many redeeming qualities. We enjoyed a most cordial discussion.'

'Really? I thought her main concern was her horse.'

'Miss Annabel is obviously very devoted to Juno.'

'Quite. I would hedge a bet she's fonder of that filly than she is of anyone else.'

Bassett cleared his throat. 'As for the household, the staff seem decent enough. Mr Jeffers is a steady sort of fellow, and as luck would have it, we follow the same football team.'

'I'm a great disappointment to you in that respect.'

'I think your tie needs a tweak, my lord. Allow me.'

'Thank you, Bassett. Ever the soul of tact.'

'As for the cook, I'm told Mrs Petts has years of experience.'

'Good show. If afternoon tea's anything to go by, we shall all be in for a treat tonight. I'm sure you'll be well fed too.' He checked his watch. 'My word, is that the time?'

'No rush, my lord. In fact, I've promised Jeffers to help him carry Miss Annabel downstairs. She can bear weight on her injured foot, but the doctor recommends lots of rest.'

'How did she get upstairs in the first place?'

'Jeffers and I were pleased to carry out the transition.'

'Were you, by Jove!'

'There's another thing I meant to say, sir — '

'While I think of it, I'm sorry you have to share the footman's room, Bassett. Very glad you're here to keep an eye on me, though. Much appreciated.'

'It is my job, sir. Life with you is never dull. Now, if I could just tell you — '

'Hmm. Nice of you and all that but, lately it's been mayhem. All that cloak and dagger business, dodging the press — total twaddle.'

'I know our stay isn't destined to be lengthy, but perhaps matters will have quietened down by the time you return to London.'

'Let's hope you're right. Mrs Crawford's given me a jolly nice room, and they seem pleasant enough, although Miss Annabel views me as lower than the lowest. So what about your quarters? Hope they haven't slotted you in with a snorer. You must have had enough of that during the war, poor chap.'

'Indeed. But as it happens, my lord, I'm billeted down the corridor in — '

'Good show.' Lawrence whirled round. 'You'd better get off then. I know you'll be a great help over these next few days, Bassett, what with one thing and another. See you later, old chap.'

★　★　★

Annabel's mother was either heeding her comment about seating plans or playing a wily game. At dinner, the daughter of the house found herself sitting between

36

her younger brother George and elder brother James. Unfortunately the visiting viscount was seated opposite, but Annabel judged his neighbours would engage him in conversation and prevent him from peering round the formidable festive centrepiece screening each of them from the other.

'I only just made it,' said George, buttering a roll. 'Ma hardly bothered to ask after my health or my journey, she was so intent on telling me about our unexpected guest.'

'What did she say?' Annabel asked him.

'Apart from reciting his illustrious pedigree? Only that he'd been let down last moment, forced to change his plans, and that Pa took pity on him. I must say, she seems rather exercised though.'

'Her trouble is, she tends to borrow inspiration from Mrs Bennett in *Pride and Prejudice*.'

'Mrs who?'

'It doesn't matter. Our mother is surveying the field for possible suitors.'

'For you?'

'No, you dunderhead — for Juno! Goodness me, Georgie, who else would she fuss about?'

'Ah. I keep thinking you're still in finishing school and interested only in four-legged creatures.'

'Well, they're usually more reliable than men.' Annabel's treacherous insides lurched as Lord Lassiter found humour in some quip of her aunt's. He possessed a laugh delicious enough to send tingles down the spine of a stone statue. Although she didn't consider him especially handsome, his eyes sparkled with intelligence and kindliness. If he wasn't such a bounder, and if she was seeking a tall, blue-eyed, golden-haired husband — which she patently wasn't — she would have been more than a little interested in becoming better acquainted.

'According to Ma, Lord Lassiter's a lawyer, but is being groomed to manage his father's Somerset estate,' said George. 'Rather him than me. I prefer working in the City to vegetating in the sticks.'

38

'So it would seem,' Annabel said.

George muttered through the side of his mouth, 'I'm rather surprised Ma's so eager to entertain him. Word is, he's not the most sought-after house guest just now; but I don't frequent his exalted circles, so really shouldn't comment.'

'Our mother makes up her own mind. You should know that by now.'

George chuckled. 'You're absolutely right. Anyway, living in London isn't only about the social whirl; it's the feeling of being at the hub of things. You should come and visit, sis. I'm sure you'd soon find someone to marry you.'

'A husband's the last thing I'm looking for. Let's make that very clear.'

On her other side, James leaned closer. 'Make what clear, little sister?'

'I was telling George that no matter what my mother or anyone else thinks, I'm not interested in potential suitors.'

Annabel's words rang out at the precise and inopportune moment the bubble of conversation burst. She watched the viscount's curly head appear around the forest of festive greenery. While her mother chimed in with what Annabel recognised as a desperate ploy to save face, by mentioning Midnight Mass at the local church, Lord Lassiter treated Annabel to a mischievous wink. Her insides melted. She lowered her gaze and wished she'd contracted an ailment. Any ailment, as long as it kept her pinned to her room, unlike the sprained ankle that allowed her to join the party and make inopportune comments.

'Well, thanks for spelling that out.' James patted her hand as the soup bowls were cleared. 'Bad luck about the ankle, Annie. At least you've plenty of strong men to carry you around.'

'Norman Bassett has helped Jeffers cart me up and downstairs. He really is a delightful gentleman.'

James looked puzzled. 'I don't see him at table.'

'Of course you don't. Mr Bassett is his lordship's valet, which means he's helping Jeffers.'

'I see. Well, that sounds a sensible

arrangement. I'm looking forward to making the viscount's acquaintance later. He seems a friendly sort of chap.'

Obviously flappers' gossip hadn't penetrated the Bristol area where her elder brother lived. Annabel fidgeted with her table napkin. Inspiration struck. 'I'm so cross I can't run round with the twins this year. It's very frustrating.'

'At least they have each other for company,' James said. 'What about reading to them or playing cards instead?'

Annabel smiled. 'I doubt they'd enjoy the kind of books I read to Great Aunt Hester. She favours the gothic novel.'

'Ah. Maybe *Through the Looking-Glass* would suit all three of them?'

'It seems my role's already mapped out. I'm becoming the perfect spinster aunt and dutiful great-niece, rolled into one.'

'What rot. Some dashing young fellow will snap you up before long. Millie thinks you've blossomed into a beauty while you've been in Switzerland.'

'Did she really say that?'

'Oh yes. Come to think of it, I bet you left a few broken hearts behind.'

'Not so loud, James. I don't want Ma suspecting anything.'

'Doesn't she realise what certain finishing schools are like?'

'Why should she? She's never set foot in one. She read all the brochures and believed every word. Fortunately Great Aunt Hester recommended the place I attended.'

'There's more to the old girl than meets the eye, don't you think?'

'All I know is that people conceal more secrets than one might imagine.'

'This smoked salmon's excellent.' James munched and swallowed. 'So has George been telling you all his secrets?'

'Hardly.' She glanced sideways. 'At the moment, he's doing an excellent job of keeping Great Aunt Hester entertained.'

'Probably coaxing her into leaving him her fortune!'

Annabel giggled. 'That's very naughty of you.'

'I know Georgie all too well. So tell

me more about your Swiss adventure. Near Lake Geneva, wasn't it?'

'Yes. Wonderful scenery, but there's not much to tell.'

'A beau or two, surely?'

She took a deep breath. 'A girl I chummed up with had a boyfriend she met at someone's house. All very proper — friends of her parents, she said. I was invited to make up a foursome and go to a party.'

'What did your chaperones say to that?'

'They knew nothing. One of the girls promised to creep down and unbolt the back door for us.'

'Did all go well?'

'We got a bit squiffy but no one found out. I enjoyed a little flirtation, shall we say.'

'Good for you. What kind of things did the tutors make you learn?

'Stupid things. They taught us how to enter and leave motorcars without show-ing too much leg. How to address a bishop and all the usual dreary stuff.'

'How to undress a bishop?'

'Stop making me laugh, James. All I need is to choke and ruin everyone's meal.'

'You won't do that. The food's always marvellous. Give Ma her due.'

'You mean she employs a good cook?'

'Touché. Is Mrs P's Emmie still here? Nice girl. Great with the twins.'

'She still works here, yes. You'd do well to make sure our brother doesn't chase after her again this year.'

'Hasn't Georgie found someone to love yet? I must have a few words.'

Annabel laid down her cutlery. 'Why is everyone so obsessed with finding love?'

She could have bitten off her tongue. Across the table, Jeffers was removing the centrepiece that might have muffled that last crass remark, undoubtedly heard by his almighty and most irritating highness, Lawrence Lassiter — even if he did look disturbingly handsome in his dinner jacket and white tie, making her ache to run her fingers through his golden curls. Maybe she'd drunk a tad too much wine.

★ ★ ★

Mrs Petts was the only person left in the kitchen when Bassett peered round the door, unable to go to his room before satisfying his curiosity.

'Hello, Phyllis. Who'd have thought we'd meet again after all these years?'

She didn't reply, only beckoned to him to sit down at the kitchen table.

'I wasn't sure you'd remember me,' he said.

'I remember you very well, Norman.'

'You're looking in the pink.'

'You too. Rather dapper, I'd say. Could hardly believe my eyes when I realised you were you.'

He cleared his throat. 'You keep a tidy ship, here. Lord Lassiter's highly impressed with your cooking.'

'I couldn't believe the kind message he sent after dinner. Mr Jeffers informed me.'

Norman nodded. 'My employer is a man of the people. It was also Mr Jeffers who told me you'd been widowed. I'm sorry to hear that. It couldn't have been easy for you, with a daughter to raise. Must say, I never thought you'd turn out to be such an accomplished cook.'

She raised her eyebrows. 'Why would you? I worked in a hospital kitchen when we first met. Peeling vegetables mostly, back then.'

'You've done extremely well, if I may say so.'

'Thank you, but life's all about changes and never giving up, don't you think?'

He held her gaze. 'I need you to know I didn't want to give you up after we got together. But I expect you remember I'd had the offer of the job in Canada. It's what I'd dreamed of. Travel. New horizons.'

'Of course I remember. But you and me — it was just the one time.'

He wrung his hands. 'It should never have worked out like it did. I should have asked you to go to Quebec with me. I fell for you, Phyllis. We'd have easily found you a position.'

'I couldn't have left home, not even if you'd gone down on bended knee with a boat ticket in one hand and a ring in the other. I couldn't even have moved as far as London. My mother's health was failing, and I'd never have slept easy at night if I'd deserted her.'

He saw within her the same fire that had attracted him in that other life. 'How did she do?'

'She hung on another twelvemonth.'

'I'm sorry.'

'My late husband was very kind to my mother and me. You might remember him from when we all attended the same church.'

'I'm glad.' Norman had no idea who she meant. His head must have been full of Canadian dreams, as well as the trim young woman with hair bright as fall maple leaves.

'At least Ma lived to see her granddaughter.'

'Mr Jeffers told me how talented Emmie is.'

'Did he, now?'

'He reckons she has it in her to go places. Find a position in a top hotel.'

'I wouldn't stand in her way.'

'She's a lucky girl, having you looking out for her.'

'I never regretted her coming along, you know.'

Norman frowned. 'Why would you? She's a credit to you.'

Phyllis looked him in the eye.

'I'm not a mind reader, you know.'

'You don't have to be. Maybe all you need's a pair of spectacles.'

'I — are you trying to tell me — ?' He leaned across the table. 'When was she born?'

'Close on Christmas 1908. She's just turned 17.'

He almost blurted out a comment he knew she'd consider tactless and tasteless, and froze as he did the sums. Could this really be true? He opened his mouth to speak. Shut it again.

Phyllis got up and reached a bottle of brandy from one of the cupboards. 'Purely medicinal.' She poured two measures into brandy goblets from a tray of glasses lined up like soldiers for a last-minute polish. 'It's not nicked from the wine cellar, in case you're wondering.'

'As if I'd think such a thing! Thank you.' It seemed inappropriate to propose a toast and his hand trembled as he raised his glass.

'Happy Christmas,' said Phyllis.

'And to you.'

Each of them took a sip. Norman felt the powerful liquid slip down his throat. Warm. Relaxing. Welcome.

'There's nothing wrong with your adding up, if that's what bothers you.' She put her glass on the table.

He did the same. 'She's mine, isn't she?'

'She's ours, Norman. Yes.'

He nodded. 'What can I say that wouldn't be intrusive or insensitive? My dear girl, why didn't you tell me?'

'Tell you I was getting married or tell

you I was carrying your child?'

He sighed and reached across to take her hands in his.

She pulled back. 'I couldn't tell you I was expecting. You must've been halfway to Canada when I knew for certain. Anyway, it wasn't like I was a silly young girl. I was well aware of what I was doing. Sam, my husband, was reliable. He paid for most of my mother's medicine. But ever since the first time you came to church, I — well, you spelled excitement. I liked seeing your eyes sparkle when you talked about your plans.'

'I can't believe how I took advantage of you like that.'

'It takes two to get carried away.' She gave a little chuckle. 'I've never forgotten that time with you, Norman Bassett.'

He groaned. 'If only I'd known. If only I'd written. Why didn't you ask for my address?'

'That would've been most unwise.'

He needed to strain to catch her quiet words. 'Why? My mother would have given it to you.'

Phyllis shook her head. 'My late husband had no reason to believe Emmie wasn't his. He thought she was a honeymoon baby. It seemed better to leave things that way. You must understand why.'

He nodded. 'When I came back to see my mother before I joined the army, I called at your house. But there were new folk living there and they didn't know where you'd gone.'

'Sam and Emmie and me — we'd moved here by then. Sam never joined up of course.'

'He'd have been needed on the home front.'

'Maybe if he'd gone away to fight, he'd have got back scot-free.'

'Like me, you mean?'

She stared at him. 'I shouldn't have said that. I'm sorry, Norman. You all had it rough out there.'

'I'm sorry too. You've been through plenty yourself.' He sat back. 'I used to think about you a lot when I was in France. Wonder where you were. What you were doing. I didn't even have a photograph to tuck in my wallet.'

'Well, now you know the story.' She glanced at the clock. 'What's done is done, and I need to be up before the birds tomorrow.'

He rose. 'I'm glad we had this chat. Thank you, Phyllis. Thanks for telling me about — about my daughter.'

She frowned. 'Emmie must never know. Maybe I shouldn't have said anything.'

'This has come as a shock, but I don't want to lose contact with you again, Phyllis. And I promise not to say a word to her, or to anyone else for that matter. I respect your confidence, and I agree that telling her would achieve nothing. Nothing at all.'

★   ★   ★

Christmas Day brought family members and the visiting viscount to breakfast at varying times. Annabel was delighted to find her foot already not quite so swollen. As soon as Mrs Petts heard of her mishap, she'd sent an arnica preparation via Jeffers. Annabel would have rubbed strawberry jam into her ankle if she thought it would make her less of an invalid.

Lawrence entered the dining room to be greeted with a chorus of Christmas greetings. 'Thank you and the same to all of you,' he said. 'Have you noticed a flake or two of snow falling?'

'Oh no!' Annabel looked around the table, avoiding his eyes. 'I hope we won't be snowed in, not with the hunt arranged for tomorrow.'

'I'm afraid the Almighty, or whoever else is in charge of the weather, won't care a fig about that,' said her father. 'Anyway, my dear, you can't possibly ride.'

Annabel narrowed her eyes. 'Twenty-four hours can make a huge difference, Pa.'

James rode to the rescue before either of his parents could utter a word. 'How did you churchgoers get on? Millie and I will take the twins to this morning's service if we can prise them away from their whips and tops and tin trumpets.'

Annabel shot him a grateful glance. Several people began talking at once and she returned to her conversation with her nephews. Out of the corner of her eye she noticed Lord Lassiter walking towards her, plate in hand, while her mother fussed over the coffee pot. Breakfast was meant to be an informal meal, but Lily Crawford had certain standards and Annabel knew it pained her to watch her noble guest tiring himself by pouring his own coffee.

'Mrs Crawford, you are kindness itself,' he said. To Annabel's dismay, he seated himself on the vacant chair beside her. 'May I? Annabel, dare I hope for your ankle to be less troublesome today?'

This time she made the mistake of meeting his gaze. Prejudice. Presumption. Disapproval. Sanity. All these vanished so long as she drowned in those forget-me-not blue eyes. She played with the muscatel grapes on her plate, terrified he'd guess her feelings. But courtesy demanded a response, especially with her mother within earshot.

'I used a preparation given me by our cook. It seems to be helping. Also, my aunt kindly bandaged my ankle up again.' She swallowed. 'Thank you for your concern.'

'If it's of help and if you'll trust me, I'll happily ride Juno to tomorrow's meet. Your father mentioned finding me a mount when we chatted before dinner last night.'

Would she trust him? Trust him with her adored, spirited chestnut? Suddenly she knew she could. He might be a full-blooded bounder, but to be fair, she still didn't know the true facts. Her new confidant, Norman, had hinted of his lordship's gentlemanly conduct, his integrity and some other virtue temporarily eluding her, given how, much to her dismay, she found herself floating on a fluffy pink cloud.

The elusive words popped into her head. Protective of a lady's reputation, that was what Norman had said. If anyone besides the man himself knew the full facts behind the broken engagement, it would be his faithful valet. Annabel resolved to wheedle this confidence out of him at the earliest opportunity.

Meanwhile, the man who'd rocked high society sat beside her, tucking into grilled bacon, kedgeree and tomatoes.

'If you're happy to ride my horse, I'm happy for you to do so,' she told him. 'But I shall be madly jealous.' She kept her eyes on her plate.

He put down his fork. Picked up his pristine linen napkin. Reached across and gently dabbed at her lower lip. Startled, she touched her fingers to her mouth.

'The merest, tiniest of crumbs. Please pardon my impertinence.' He held her gaze. 'Thank you for giving me your permission. You've agreed to trust me with something very precious to you. Please rest assured I shall take special care of Juno.'

* * *

56

Lawrence strode towards his bedroom window. Strode back again. Set off a second time, to stand, arms folded, gazing at the rolling downs of Wiltshire. The snow might have fizzled away before it began but that shouldn't apply to his reasoning powers. His recent romantic shenanigans were a life lesson. Those first heady days with Lucinda catapulted him from jolly bachelor to devoted fiancé ridiculously fast. He'd been gullible. His friends assured him debutantes' mothers in London and the shires considered him a good catch. He found this embarrassing but doubtless true, if all you cared about were blood-lines and a family pile. Lucinda's parents decided he'd make a suitable husband for their glamorous daughter. He was too besotted to add two and two.

Lucinda's parents didn't bargain on their daughter becoming infatuated with an older man she met at a party the Prince of Wales hosted. Lawrence was away on business, and it didn't do the young viscount's confidence any good to learn of his fiancée being seen in compromising circumstances. Thanks to his decision to shoulder the responsibility for Lucinda's change of heart, her behaviour still remained a scandal waiting to hit the society column headlines. Maybe when it did, his perceived boorishness would be understood by all, and more importantly, forgotten.

He'd survive. He didn't begrudge Lucinda the alibi provided in order to spare her blushes. What they'd shared wasn't love. He knew that now. What he did begrudge was how Annabel found it so difficult to deal with him. She was six years younger than he was — a debutante in love with life, with her horse and her twin nephews. She intrigued him, but to this beautiful young lady black was black and white was white. Her chilliness indicated she viewed him as a piece of pond life. He so wanted to prove otherwise to her, though the force of this urge concerned him. Was he totally beyond hope?

Hearing a discreet tap, he swung round.

'Pardon me, my lord, but I wanted to bring your eveningwear upstairs, out of the way.'

'Busy down there, I imagine, Bassett?'

'Yes, but in a good way, sir.'

'Have you ever been in love, Bassett?'

'That's a strange question.'

'I know. I've never posed it to anyone before, and that concerns me.'

Bassett didn't reply. But a little smile played around his lips as he moved to the wardrobe and hung the impeccably pressed shirt and suit inside.

'The trouble is, I'm experiencing a feeling I never, ever felt with you-know-who. It's nothing like that exhilarating, up-in-the-clouds whirligig of before. It's more like a coming-home feeling, but better. I mean, it's exciting, but in a different way from — from the Lucinda feeling.'

'I see.'

'As one might expect, the young lady in question knows only such facts as I saw fit to trot out to her father. Consequently she views me with as much favour as she'd give a week-old fillet of sole.'

'Surely not, my lord?'

'Oh, I think so.' Lawrence managed an apologetic smile. 'There's no one else I can confide in but you, old chap. Most of my friends, and unquestionably my parents, view me as a dead loss just now; and if I even hinted I'd fallen for another girl, I'd be laughed out of town, don't you think?'

'With respect, my lord, none of the aforementioned folk are in the vicinity.'

'Something to be thankful for, I suppose.' Lawrence began striding back and forth again.

'Christmas can be an emotional time, sir. It's when families gather, so maybe you miss your own loved ones more than you realise.'

Lawrence stopped striding. 'Goodness. So you think I should ignore these worrisome feelings?'

'If it's any help, and if the object of your lordship's affections is the young lady I assume it is, I think you should credit her with the wit to recognise your true character, even if it takes a while longer than you'd wish.'

'That is sensible advice, Bassett, much as I'd expect from an upright fellow like you.' He consulted his watch. 'I'd better get a shift on. Having not made it last night, better not miss the service this morning.'

'I was about to remind you, my lord.' Bassett disappeared into the adjoining dressing room, to emerge carrying Lawrence's Crombie overcoat, trilby hat, muffler and gloves.

'So, Bassett, did you attend Midnight Mass as you thought you might? I forgot to enquire last night.'

'I didn't, my lord. But I got to know one or two members of the staff a little better.'

'Good for you. I decided to keep Great Aunt Hester company. She's formidable, but quite a character. Doesn't seem in the least bit bothered about my recent predicament.'

Bassett helped Lawrence into his

coat. 'It's possible the good lady may be unaware of the incident, sir.'

'Well it's good to know that at least one female doesn't consider me a scallywag.'

'Oh, I think Miss Annabel's mother would hardly label you as such, my lord.'

The valet opened the door for the viscount. Lawrence hurried downstairs, leaving Norman to his thoughts. Christmas was indeed the time to think of family. How ironic it was to be spending the festive season in the same house as Phyllis Petts — his Phyllis, as he still thought of her — as well as a daughter he never knew he'd possessed. Ironic indeed, because he had no right to regard either of them as family; and this realisation wrapped him round with a heavy black cloud of regret.

★ ★ ★

Mrs Petts gazed around at what she often likened to a stage. She of course took the central role, supported by Emmie and Violet. Today Norman Bassett and the footman would help Mr Jeffers wait on family and guests, but she mustn't think about Norman. Not when she had oysters to grill without turning the delicate shellfish to chewy rubber.

Mock turtle soup simmered on the hob. The seafood platter rested on a marble slab in the pantry. Beef Wellington, a crisp pastry crust concealing the moist meat, rested in the slow oven, while in the big oven a stuffed goose roasted. Soon its golden-brown skin would crackle and yield to the carving knife's sharp blade. Phyllis had prepared Brussels sprouts with chestnuts, braised red cabbage and apple, and the usual root vegetables. A gigantic plum pudding steamed gently, while Emmie's Buche de Noel and fresh fruit salad waited in the wings with her marzipan fruits, miniature meringues and brandy truffles. The pungent scent of sizzling garlic butter filled the kitchen.

Emmie hovered with two serving dishes

to hand. The cook turned around as soon as the juicy oysters curled at the edges. 'Here we go, Emmie.' She removed the huge grill pan from the heat. 'First batch coming up.'

So began the production line. Pans removed. Pans added. Staff instructed. Vegetables drained. Gravy stirred. Faces flushed with heat.

'I think that Mr Bassett's really nice,' said Emmie after she and her mother saw the men set off with the goose and all its trimmings. 'Funny how he really did turn out old enough to be my father.'

Phyllis felt her heart beat faster. 'Has he been speaking with you?'

'Only to thank me for dishing up breakfast.'

'Serving his breakfast, Emmie. And don't go muttering under your breath. I'm only trying to help you not sound like a country bumpkin.'

'Whatever for?'

Her daughter's indignant expression made Phyllis laugh. 'It's important to speak well nowadays, silly. Times are changing. You won't always want to work as a kitchen maid, will you?'

Emmie gasped. She lifted a lid. 'They've forgotten to take in the devils on horseback. See?'

'Oh my word — and thirteen at table today! Let's hope nothing else goes wrong. Take them through to Mr Jeffers or — or Mr Bassett, whoever's closer.'

'Can't Violet go?'

Phyllis placed the serving dish on a tray. 'Move. Say nothing and pray the old lady hasn't noticed her favourites are missing. Given half a chance, she'd wolf the lot, according to Mr Jeffers.' Emmie nodded and did as she was asked.

Phyllis sank down on the chair beside the range. She'd not noticed before, but now, with Emmie and her real father in her sights, she could see clearly how her daughter resembled him. What if someone else noticed? Would they shrug it off as coincidence? Thank goodness for those fiery curls inherited from her side.

She reminded herself Norman Bassett would be leaving in a matter of days. Seeing him again stirred old memories and unlocked feelings kept hidden for years.

But now wasn't the time for restless thoughts. Phyllis saw Violet give her a curious look as the girl carried yet another load of dirty plates to the sink. 'Cheer up, Vi. We'll have extra pairs of hands for the party tomorrow.'

'I don't know how you stay so cheerful, Mrs P, and that's a fact. My hands get so red and sore.'

'Think about the nice meal we'll be eating later, soon as everything's sorted in the dining room. Mr Crawford always comes through and pours us each a glass of wine.'

'Even me?'

'Even you, Vi. Miss Annabel likes to help wait on us, but she won't be doing that today. Not with that gammy ankle.'

Violet summoned up a smile. 'I'm glad I works here, Mrs Petts. A friend of mine's a skivvy somewhere there's a right old dragon of a cook.'

'I shan't comment, Vi. Always remember the post goes two ways.'

★ ★ ★

Lawrence decided that if he closed his eyes, he'd still know it was Christmas. That combination of Scots pine, candle wax, roasted meats and cinnamon was unmistakable. He was enjoying his day far more than he imagined he would after accepting George Crawford's invitation. By some magical means, each of the twins had discovered a shiny silver sixpence in their portion of pudding. Lawrence suspected the family cook of masterminding this trick, and he also approved the idea of the boys joining the grown-ups in the dining room. His relations mostly hid their young offspring in the nursery.

He'd eaten as well as he could have at his family home or at that of his former fiancée, and to his surprise found the company jollier. He'd laughed to hear of a prank George Junior confided to him, but on realising what his host was saying, turned his attention to it.

'I shall of course do my usual stint for the staff meal,' said Mr Crawford.

Lawrence missed hearing what the vicar asked George Crawford, but the reply was perfectly audible and provided food for thought.

'I help serve them at table. Pour them all a glass of wine and thank them for their hard work. Usually, my daughter helps pass the food round and so forth, but not this time of course.'

Those seated close enough to hear made sympathetic noises. Lawrence wondered if the vicar was debating whether to offer assistance or whether to stay put in case he missed another round of food. He chided himself over such an uncharitable sentiment. He was the usurper, and definitely shouldn't harbour such feelings towards a man of the cloth. Suddenly he thought what fun it might be to take Annabel's place. Ignoring the possibility of any ulterior motive, he took a deep breath.

'I wonder whether I might help you, Mr Crawford. It's the least I can do when you're welcoming me into your home and entertaining me so royally. I couldn't have wished for a more mouth-watering dinner, enjoyed in such congenial company.' He noticed Lily Crawford beaming, though her husband looked a little concerned.

'There's really no need, Lord Lassiter. It's an honour to have you staying.'

'Please call me Lawrence. I have no wish to stand on ceremony.'

'Pa?' Annabel obviously had ears like a lynx. She also possessed a hard stare, now focused firmly upon her father. 'I think you should accept his lordship's kind offer.'

George Crawford harrumphed. 'My daughter imagines she can wind me round her little finger, Lawrence. I wouldn't dream of imposing.'

'But you wouldn't be. I meant what I said. Besides, my valet will be highly entertained by the proceedings.'

George Crawford laughed. 'In that case, how could I possibly refuse? They usually sit down at seven o'clock. There'll be a cold spread laid on the sideboard in here and we won't be away long.'

Lawrence noticed the vicar's eyes gleam. Without doubt, the old boy was in heaven. He longed to share the quip with Annabel.

'I can't imagine even looking a biscuit in the face again; but please, when you're ready, let me know. I don't expect I'll be far away.'

His gaze strayed towards Annabel. She averted her eyes, but to his immense delight immediately sneaked another peek. How wonderful if she'd been checking whether he was still gazing at her.

After the meal, gifts were exchanged. Lawrence had specifically asked that people shouldn't worry about gifts for their extra guest, but two or three packages emerged from beneath the tree for him. He'd asked his valet to buy boxes of chocolates and bottles of port to go around the assembled company. This squeezed a smile from the crotchety vicar, especially when he discovered Lawrence was an amateur cricketer and had watched the famous Mr Jack Hobbs play in a match the previous summer.

Electric lamps helped the candlelight as day dissolved into dusk. Just after seven, Mr Jeffers informed Mr Crawford the staff were assembled. On their way to the kitchen, Lawrence learnt a little about how the household was run.

'In their own room they take turns to make up the fire,' George Crawford explained. 'When they're not on duty they can sit there, rather than hang around the kitchen or their bedrooms.'

'If I may say so, sir, you have a very enlightened view when it comes to dealings with servants. I find it most refreshing.'

'I wish you'd call me George, my boy.' Inside the kitchen, the master greeted Mrs Petts and Emmie. A buzz of conversation rose from the happy staff.

'Another magnificent feast, ladies,' said Mr Crawford. 'As might be expected, everything was of a very high standard indeed.'

'Indeed it was,' said Lawrence. He smiled at the cook and her daughter. 'Thank you very much.'

'I'm glad you were pleased, sir.' Phyllis bobbed smoothly. 'Thank you too, my lord.'

'Let's serve the wine. Are you ready to sit down, Mrs Petts?'

'I am, sir, thank you. The soup's already on the table.'

'Then after you, ladies.' He waved them forward.

Lawrence was agreeably surprised by the cosiness of the servants' sitting room. A dark green chenille cloth covered the long table. Sprigs of scarlet-berried holly and white-painted fir cones were dotted about, with a festive cracker beside each place.

The master poured wine and Lawrence handed glasses around. Swiftly, Mr Jeffers proposed a toast. 'To Mr Crawford! The finest employer in the county.'

Everyone echoed the sentiment.

Lawrence glanced at his valet. Mrs Petts had taken the seat next to him; and as the viscount noticed the cook's bright curls, released from their usual cap, he intercepted a look between her and Norman. What was that about? He'd never seen fit to question Bassett about his personal life, though he knew much about his background and how he'd fought for his country. But he'd never have put the fellow down as a fast worker with the ladies. In fact, he never enquired what his valet got up to on days off. Still waters often ran deep. Lawrence concentrated on helping Violet and Tommy pass dinner plates around while his host doled out succulent slices of meat.

★　★　★

On the morning of Boxing Day, Lawrence rang for his valet to help him dress in his riding habit. 'How's the weather looking, Bassett? I'm grateful you made the fire up last night.'

'It's still gloomy out there, sir. Some windowpanes are iced inside, I noticed.'

'Oh dear. Let's hope the snow holds off.'

'The fox will hope for a good covering, no doubt, my lord.'

'Hmm. I'm partly on the side of Reynard, as you know. There must be something about my personality preventing me from offending people who feel strongly that blood sports are important.'

'I believe you enjoy the tradition and the convivial atmosphere, my lord.'

'Indeed I do, Bassett. Just as I hope you enjoyed last night's Christmas dinner with the new friends you've made.' He noticed Norman's eyes gleam.

'Yes indeed, and may I say how much everyone appreciated your attendance, my lord? You were rated a more than adequate substitute for Miss Annabel.'

'Praise indeed. Now, I must go and see if I'm still allowed to ride Juno.'

Lawrence loped downstairs and entered the dining room to find Annabel and her father already at table.

'You're up and about early, my boy.' Mr Crawford extended his hand.

'Please don't let me disturb your breakfast, George. Good morning to you both.'

'I hope you're looking forward to riding the Irish filly?'

Lawrence helped himself to eggs and bacon. Mr Jeffers swiftly filled his coffee cup. 'I am indeed, George. May I ask how your ankle's feeling today, Annabel?'

'Better, thank you. I'm hoping another two or three days will see me back in the saddle.'

'I shall do my absolute best to remain in mine.'

Mr Crawford chuckled. 'Juno's a docile enough horse if you know what you're doing, Lawrence, and I have to say we have an excellent hunt master.' He sipped his tea. 'We should be in for a splendid day, as long as snow threatens rather than falls.'

'It would be disappointing if the weather spoilt proceedings,' said Lawrence.

'I'm so annoyed I can't take part. I wonder if I could join the hunt followers,' said Annabel.

Lawrence inclined his head. She'd caught him with his mouth full of toast but his host rescued him.

'Over my dead body, young lady! Didn't the doctor advise you to rest your foot?'

'But the swelling's all but vanished, Pa, and I fear my brain will explode if I have to read Great Aunt Hester even one more paragraph of *Wuthering Heights*. As for those interminable card games with those silly little red and black symbols . . .'

Lawrence kept his gaze on his willow-pattern plate, though he found difficulty in restraining a smile.

'I still recommend you stay put this morning, Annabel. Please let that be an end to the matter.'

She was saved by the arrival of more family members. Lawrence wondered who would ultimately win the argument. Something about the pretty debutante's tilted chin hinted at a Boudicca dressed for battle beneath that attractive exterior.

★   ★   ★

Accompanied by his host and Annabel's brother James, Lawrence revelled in the cold snap and the prospect of a good gallop. The hunt members gathered outside a nearby hostelry, taking a cup of mulled wine to warm the cockles while Mr Crawford took the opportunity to introduce his guest to his friends, all of whom were attending the party at the manor house later. Two or three riders looked bemused on hearing his full title, but Lawrence felt he'd got off pretty lightly.

Then, crossing a field, hounds panting, horses galloping at full tilt, his breath white smoke merging with Juno's, he noticed the unmistakeably tall, bowler-hated figure of his valet standing beyond the low wall separating field from highway. Nor was Norman Bassett unescorted. Beside him stood a woman wearing a camel-hair overcoat, her shiny dark hair concealed by a crimson felt cloche hat, but unmistakeably Annabel. She was gripping the top bar of the gate with both gloved hands.

Lawrence's groan of longing melted into the cacophony of men shouting and hounds baying. He pretended he hadn't noticed her, but knew Bassett must have driven the Bentley and would only have done so because she'd coaxed him. The impudence of her!

Yet he hoped her father hadn't spotted her, even though she was no longer a child. Her impetuous nature both astonished and attracted Lawrence, too accustomed to simpering girls and predatory young ladies — to which latter category he realised his former fiancée belonged.

★　★　★

Bassett helped Lawrence off with his jacket. 'With respect, my lord, I didn't consider the request unreasonable under the circumstances.'

'Is that so? Did she not tell you her father expressly forbade her to follow on foot? Understandably, he didn't wish her to aggravate her lame state.' Lawrence didn't wait for an answer. 'You were with me when we helped her on Christmas Eve. You're clearly much more in favour than I am, even though she entrusted me with her beloved horse today. Didn't you suspect she was taking advantage of the soft spot you have for her by asking you to steal my car and drive her to watch the hunt?'

Lawrence watched a slow blush suffuse his valet's cheeks. He'd trust Norman with his life and he'd lend him the Bentley without a second thought, but he was cross with him for colluding with Annabel. Jealous, even.

'Mr Bassett, that young woman shouldn't have tried walking more than a few steps. Who knows but between the pair of you if you haven't put back her recovery by several days? Perhaps damaged her ankle permanently!'

'I can assure you the young lady did not have occasion to bear her weight, negligible as it is, while under my care, sir.'

Lawrence's eyebrows shot up. 'Did someone provide a bath chair? Stop trying to pull the wool over my eyes.'

'I carried Miss Annabel from the sitting room to the back door of the domestic quarters, where she rested in a chair provided by, um, one of the staff.'

'That would be the magnificent Mrs Petts, I presume. Another of your conquests.'

He saw the gleam of appreciation in the older man's eyes and suspected his valet was enjoying the sparring as much as he was.

'Miss Annabel and I had already, um, hatched a plan,' said Bassett, holding out a clean shirt. 'While I moved the Bentley closer to the back door, two of the lads carried her outside and helped her into the back seat, so she could sit with both her — well, without having to keep her feet on the floor.'

'She would of course know exactly where to find an excellent view of the hunt. No doubt you were able to carry her the short distance from the car to the grass verge.'

'Indeed, my lord.'

But Lawrence could no longer keep up his onslaught. Peals of laughter rang out while he watched his valet's face contort as he tried to maintain his decorum. 'Don't worry, Norman. I shan't sneak on the pair of you. I don't think our host noticed, and if he did, he's keeping it under his hat.'

'Thank you, sir. I apologise if my behaviour seemed in any way inappropriate.'

'Truth is, Bassett, Miss Annabel could charm the coins from a beggar's bowl. I'm not surprised she tugged at your heartstrings. Let's hope that's the end of it. She shouldn't have involved you, but I understand it must have been difficult for you to refuse, given we're guests of this family.'

Famished by exercise and frosty air, Lawrence descended to the dining room where he received a warm welcome. The rest of the family, apart from Annabel and her father, had already eaten.

'Come and sit down, dear boy,' said Mr Crawford. 'I was just telling my daughter what a good morning we had. Top marks for acquitting yourself so well.'

'I should also say that one of the maids told me they enjoyed meeting you last night. I gather you gained a round of applause,' said Annabel.

Lawrence, admiring the swift subject change, took the seat opposite her and ladled oxtail soup into his bowl. 'You're very kind, both of you. It was good to see your staff enjoying themselves, and I know Mr Bassett was made to feel welcome. As for today, all credit should go to a certain lady. She's really rather wonderful. Beautiful, too. Definitely a spirited filly who needs firm handling, but with such very satisfactory results.'

The words were addressed to George Crawford, but the viscount's gaze held Annabel's. He felt tremendous satisfaction seeing her cheeks turn a fetching shade of pink before she switched her attention to her bread roll and butter.

*　　*　　*

Annabel faced a dilemma. She daren't risk dancing even one step when the party moved into the big reception room where musicians held court. But could she really face joining Aunt Hester and her cronies on the sidelines?

She stared at her reflection in the dressing-table mirror. There would be young women at the party whom she knew and in some cases whose company she enjoyed. There could even be a young man or two who'd seek her out and keep her champagne glass filled.

The most disturbing thing of all was how much her attitude had changed towards the viscount. This began even before her little jaunt with his valet provided the perfect opportunity to press Norman into disclosing the events leading to the end of Lord Lassiter's betrothal.

Annabel's problem lay in allowing

her former chilliness to Lawrence to melt away. He'd surely wonder at this change of heart and might suspect her of coaxing confidential information from his faithful servant. She hated the thought of Norman coming under fire for indiscretion.

Yet, to maintain her froideur, to quote one of her great-aunt's favourite expressions, and stay distanced from a man who'd smashed through her original perceptions simply by being himself, didn't appeal. Any gentleman prepared to place his reputation on the line to protect his perfidious former fiancée must possess a steadfastness Annabel found sadly lacking in most of the men her mother considered husband material.

But the viscount was way out of Annabel's league, and her mother should realise it. Norman had said only good things about his employer and Annabel trusted his judgement. Sadly, the picture painted of Lucinda and her scandalous behaviour was an eye-opener. She promised herself that if any guest spotted the viscount and began spreading vile rumours, she would put paid to such mischief in no uncertain manner.

This decision calmed her. As to how she would accomplish this, given that she'd be lying around like Cleopatra on her barge, was a different matter. Not even Great Aunt Hester had reached the bath chair stage, so Annabel would need to lurk in a corner where she'd be available but not in anyone's way. The only consolation was not being required to dance with drippy youths, most of them more concerned with their own images than with interesting things like horses, cars and aeroplanes.

Her mother employed a young woman from the nearby village to take care of her wardrobe and help dress her hair for social engagements. Earlier, Annabel's own hair had been styled not tortured, so catching sight of her reflection in the looking glass didn't displease her, especially as her dress, a symphony of pinks, clung and swung in all the right places. Shoes were a problem until her mother, who took a size larger than Annabel, produced a pair of white satin slippers. For the first time since Christmas Eve, she would tackle stairs, even if on the arm of her brother, George.

When she heard a knock, she invited him to enter, before rising to face the door. She almost sat straight down again.

'How beautiful you are, Annabel.' The viscount walked towards her. 'Permit me to escort you to the party. George is entertaining your nephews with a thrilling tale of pirates, sharks and treasure troves. So I'm here in his place.'

'Goodness.' She swallowed hard. 'That's a side of him I've never seen.'

'People are not always what we perceive,' Lawrence spoke softly.

Annabel's heart somersaulted. She'd never been one to swoon over handsome young men; but seeing this one beside her, so close, and with such a tender expression on his face, she knew the futility of fighting her feelings.

'My mother would swoon if she knew you were alone with me in my bedroom.'

'Am I in danger, Annabel? I do hope so.' His blue eyes sparkled.

They faced each other. She should take his arm and begin walking. Instead, she placed both hands lightly upon his broad shoulders and tilted her face up-wards. His lips were close. So very close. She shut her eyes. Hoped he couldn't hear the thumping of her heart. *This*, she thought, *is what I want*.

'Annabel!' Footsteps treading the land-ing. A voice calling from outside her door. She turned abruptly. Lawrence put his arm around her waist in support.

'What is it?' she called.

Her elder brother stood in the door-way. 'Forgive me for interrupting, but I have a message for you, Lawrence.'

'For me? Who is it from, James?'

'Your former fiancée has arrived and is, erm, demanding to see you.'

Lawrence winced. 'Lucinda's here? You mean she's gate-crashed your party?'

James hurried forward. 'You'd better go down to her ladyship. I'll make sure my sister descends in one piece.'

Lawrence relaxed his hold on Annabel. She felt bereft. So many questions remained unanswered, and she could only imagine his anguish.

He shot her a pleading look. 'I'm sorry, Annabel. I have no idea what's brought about this astonishingly rude behaviour.'

'It's best you do as James suggests, my lord.'

The look of desolation in Lawrence's eyes left her yearning to reach out to him. But the story she suspected might have been beginning seemed fated to remain untold.

★　★　★

On entering Mrs Crawford's bijou sitting room, Lawrence was met by an all-too-familiar exotic scent. He closed the door behind him. 'What's this about, Lucinda? Have you no shame?'

'Dear Lawrence, always so passionate about what's right and what's wrong. It's splendid to see you, but do try and keep your voice down, darling.' Lady Lucinda smiled up at him from the crimson velvet settee.

'Any idiot would know how wrong it is to turn up here uninvited.'

'Really! I'll have you know I'm here as the guest of one of George Crawford's friends. I'm staying in the area for a night or two. You know Charlie Bell? He's thrilled to bits having me on his arm.'

'Good for him. He always was a chump. How on earth did you know I was here?'

'I have my spies, darling.'

'I don't understand. Where's the actor?'

She sighed. 'Everett Hastings was merely a passing fancy, Lawrence. I mistakenly believed I'd fallen in love. We were both carried away, but such a little fling is commonplace nowadays. You must rea-lise that. You reacted in such haste, didn't you?'

He shook his head.

She pouted. 'Surely you're pleased to see me? Forgive and forget so things can return to normal?' She unleashed one of her seductive looks, the kind that used to nail him to the floor. Now he felt only distaste.

'You are, I'm afraid, sadly mistaken,' said Lawrence. 'I have endured much embarrassment since your 'little fling', as you regard it, ended our engagement. Tongues will wag tonight, Lucinda, and who could blame people for gossiping? For the life of me, I can't understand why you want to turn up here, when you could be dancing the night away at some house party with the prince and his crowd.'

'Because, idiot boy, I want you and I to become engaged again. My mother was right, we're perfect for each other, so don't be huffy. You know I can't bear it when you're angry.' She gazed up at him with violet eyes fringed with lavish lashes. Her lips, painted bright scarlet, parted slightly.

'I'm not angry. Merely puzzled as to why, after all the chaos you brought into my life, you have the audacity to think I'm willing to renew our engagement

— a betrothal I've since realised should never have occurred.'

She sighed. 'You can't really mean that. Your pride was wounded and you're getting your own back. It's all right. I completely understand. Can you pass me a cigarette, my darling?'

'No. Can't you understand I have nothing more to say? Except that I've no intention of making you my viscountess.'

She glanced at the exquisite diamond watch on her left wrist. 'We've been closeted together a while. People will wonder what we're up to, my sweet. Stop being so stubborn and come and sit over here.'

'Contrary to what you might believe, I'd rather kiss one of George Crawford's horses than lower myself to embrace you.'

Her eyes narrowed. 'You're unhappy. That's why you're saying such spiteful things. After supper, I insist you dance with me so everyone can see how civilised we are. They'll be thrilled to see us together again. Remember those gossip column headlines?' Her expression became coy. 'The golden couple, Lawrence and his lovely Lucinda.'

He shook his head. 'You sicken me.'

Finally accepting that her charms were having no effect on him, Lucinda dropped the pretence of civility, and her eyes flashed furiously. 'Damn you, Lawrence Lassiter. You'll regret this.'

'My only regret is that you didn't do me this favour sooner. You only ever wanted me for my title. Why don't you admit what you know is true?'

They glared at each other. He wondered what on earth he'd ever seen in her as he watched her shimmy off the sofa and stand upright.

'I think this slumming you're indulging in, staying here with the vulgar Crawford family, has made you forget your manners. That alone will make a tasty titbit for the newspapers, my sweet, don't you think? Your dear parents will be incandescent. Do they even know where you're spending Christmas?'

Lawrence's nails bit into his palms.

When someone tapped at the door, Lucinda snapped at him, 'Tell whoever it is to scram. I haven't finished with you yet.'

But the door opened and Lawrence had never before been so pleased to see Norman Bassett, immaculate and implacable and immensely reassuring. The valet bowed in Lucinda's direction. 'Forgive the interruption, your ladyship, but I have been instructed to inform Lord Lassiter that supper is being served.'

Lawrence breathed a fervent sigh of relief. 'May I enquire as to who sent you, Bassett?'

Norman held his head high. 'Why, the young lady to whom you have so recently become betrothed, my lord. I believe Miss Annabel is anxious to introduce you to her circle of friends.'

★   ★   ★

Norman Bassett closed the door behind him and gazed up at the stars. Inside, the kitchen buzzed with energy as staff juggled empty plates and squirreled away leftovers, the washers-up slaved at the vast sink, and Mrs Petts supervised the despatching of trays of delicacies.

Again he pictured the expression on the Lady Lucinda's face as he dropped his bombshell. Her reaction had exceeded his wildest dreams. He held his own opinion of her ladyship, one he didn't intend to divulge. He wasn't normally prone to eavesdropping, but hearing the desperation in his employer's voice as he passed the sitting-room door, he'd glanced around to make sure no one was nearby and pretended to retie his shoelace.

The viscount's reaction to this most unladylike of ladies persuaded Norman to act swiftly. He'd tapped on the door and told a lie, even if a well-intentioned one. His employer had looked relieved, especially as Norman gave him the ghost of a wink without his unwelcome visitor noticing.

This declaration set several things in

motion. Lady Lucinda had collapsed on the crimson cushions, wailing in misery. Or anger. His lordship had asked Bassett to fetch a glass of water. Lady Lucinda promptly stopped bawling and requested something stronger. Bassett had hurried off to fetch not only a glass of champagne but also the lady's escort, though this gentleman was appalled to be deprived of such a sumptuous supper.

The viscount shook hands with a disgruntled Charlie Bell, thanked him for attending, and informed him his partner was indisposed. While this was unfortunate, it was best if the couple left at once. Bassett promptly fetched their outer garments before hurrying outside to find Mr Bell's chauffeur, who was hanging around in the barn with the other drivers.

Lord Lassiter saw the couple off the premises before turning to his valet. 'My bacon, as they say, has been saved. But I don't believe for one moment Miss Annabel sent that message.'

'My lord?'

'The idea is, of course, ludicrous.'

'If you say so, sir.'

'Does anyone else know about it?'

'Of course not, my lord.'

Lord Lassiter shook his head slowly. 'Whatever shall I do if news of this second engagement leaks out, Norman? I'll be a laughing stock, and I dread to think what Miss Annabel will say. I'd be grateful to receive the advice of the instigator of this announcement.'

'You should follow the advice of your heart, my lord.'

Lord Lassiter stared back at him in silence, until a smile of dawning light mixed with joy split his face. He clapped his valet upon the back. 'You are, as usual, absolutely right, my friend. Thank you. Now I must rejoin the party.'

Norman watched his employer hurry to the dining room. The gathering consisted of only fifty or so folk, but much care had been taken to create a scrumptious buffet. The revellers wore evening dress, the ladies' gorgeous gowns and jewels adding their colours to those radiated by the room's décor and glittering decorations.

Suddenly he felt a waft of warm air as the door opened behind him. He swung around.

'You trying to catch your death?' Phyllis handed him a cup of mulled wine. He wrapped his fingers around its warmth.

'You're an angel, Phyllis Petts. As if you haven't enough to do.'

'I saw you come out here. All my hard work's done for the night, so I thought I'd check up on you and leave the others to it.'

He offered her his cup. 'Take a sip or two. I can't drink alone.'

'I wouldn't normally offer alcohol when you're on duty, but it seemed a good idea under the circumstances.'

'Might I ask what you've heard?'

'Only that Lord Lassiter's former fiancée turned up escorted by a gentleman. The footman whispered it to me.'

'He'd have let them in, of course.'

'He told me the lady who's related to the Prince of Wales had turned up. Said she looked like a film star with her blonde curls, and all dressed up to the nines in white with fur coat to match.'

'Did he mention she smelled like Harrods' perfume department? Who else knows, Phyllis?'

'Don't worry. I told him to keep it to himself unless he wanted to live on bread and water till Twelfth Night.'

'You're a treasure, you really are.'

'I imagine this has made life difficult for his lordship, but I understand if you'd prefer not to tell me anything.' She always did have a nice way of speaking, much more refined than most women Norman worked with in the past, unless they were governesses or ladies' maids.

'Let's just say I needed my wits about me to prevent an awkward situation from worsening,' he said. 'We're not quite out of the woods yet though, Phyllis. Some people can be very vindictive.'

'Not you, Norman. Definitely not you.'

'It's good of you to say so. Especially to the man who quit your life, leaving you in the lurch.'

She touched his arm briefly. 'I told you, we can't bring back the past. I took the plunge and married someone else, to give our daughter a name. She's been well looked after, Norman. By her dad and by me.'

'That's very clear, Phyllis. You've done a good job. But now I've found you, I want to do my bit.'

'I think you already have!'

He chuckled. 'I want to help give her the chance to better herself.' He glanced at Phyllis' face. 'Now, don't go taking umbrage. I know what kind of money she'll be earning here. I've got a tidy stash in the bank, and I'd like to give some to you so you can use it whichever way you think fit.'

'Thank you, but it's not necessary.'

'Don't you believe she could do better than being a kitchen maid in a country house?'

'Of course. She's a bright girl. I've

been teaching her what I can, but I can't give her my job, now can I?'

'Certainly not. But with you training her, and me providing the cash for her to travel and stay somewhere respectable when she has interviews lined up, she'll stand an excellent chance of obtaining a position in a London hotel.'

'That's what you told me Mr Jeffers thought. You don't know for sure.'

'Don't underestimate his opinion. Since he said that, I've been keeping my eyes and ears open. I've heard a lot of compliments about the quality of the meals produced in this kitchen, and I know who's responsible, don't I?'

She hesitated. 'She's still so young.'

'Emmie's seventeen. She understands the importance of good food. If she's keen to enter the catering trade, it's high time she became apprenticed.'

'I know I said I'd not stand in her way, but I hate to think of her all alone in London.'

'She'd be working with other youngsters finding their feet. She'll make friends, don't you fret. And if she lands a job at an establishment right in the heart of things, well, his lordship's townhouse is where I spend a lot of my time. I know plenty of people working around the West End. With your permission, I'd be glad to keep an eye on her. Take her out to tea now and then. Between Emmie and me, we could keep you posted about her progress.'

'You'd write letters to me?'

He swallowed. 'I could write the kind of letters I used to dream of writing to you, Phyllis, all those years ago in Canada, far from home and learning how to survive those sub-zero winters.'

* * *

Lawrence bit his lip and looked at Annabel. 'Luckily it's still not snowing. That really would have been most unpleasant for Lucinda.'

'You're a kind man, Lawrence,' she said. 'Plenty of people in your position would have tried to shame her, despite her royal connection.'

'At least you know all the pieces of the jigsaw now. I might have known Bassett would spill the beans.'

'For some reason he seems to like me. I hope you won't be cross with him.'

Lawrence smiled. 'I shan't. I never could see the point of being vindictive, Annabel, whoever might have it in for me. But I'm afraid Lucinda might be tempted to blacken my name. She'd better not try the same trick with you, though!'

'I'm sure people who really care about you won't take a scrap of notice. As for Norman, what a treasure that man is. What incredible loyalty he showed this evening.'

'Yes indeed. Obviously we could do without more gossip reaching the press, but he certainly saved me from a sticky situation.'

'If I were Lady Lucinda, I'd keep jolly quiet about everything,' Annabel laughed. 'She can only make herself look foolish, don't you think?'

'I suppose. And I'm very glad you are who you are and not Lady Lucinda. I sincerely hope I need never see her again.'

'I doubt you can avoid that. Best to keep your dragon slayer close by, don't you think?'

He chuckled. 'He'd appreciate that. You're such fun to be with, Annabel.'

'I can't help thinking that if her ladyship had turned up and found you ready and willing to let bygones be bygones, she'd have cut a very romantic and glamorous figure in the gossip columns. She is very beautiful.'

Lawrence grinned wryly. 'On the surface, maybe. I can't believe the nerve of the woman. But let's forget her. I'm relieved you know the reason why I've been viewed as such a reprobate.'

Annabel avoided his eyes. She sat back and stared at the toes of the white satin slippers peeping from her gown's rosy folds. 'I never thought the day would come when I'd be glad to borrow a pair of my mother's shoes.'

'You look so stunning that I doubt anyone with eyes in their head will have given your footwear a second glance.'

'Thank you. I need to tell you I'm sorry for my chilly manner towards you.'

'No one could blame you for feeling affronted.'

'I was relieved to hear the truth, but it's a lesson to me not to heed gossip.' She paused. 'It would have been lovely to dance with you tonight, Lawrence. I doubt there'll be another chance.'

'Please don't say that. Now that you know the truth behind my so-called disgraceful behaviour, I hope we might become friends. There's not that great a distance between our fathers' estates, you know.'

She stared into the fire. 'I know we inhabit different worlds.'

A dozen or so people still lingered, chatting and drinking at the other end of the room, though the dancing was finished and most guests had gone home.

'I don't understand,' Lawrence said, looking at Annabel quizzically.

'I surely don't need to spell it out. My family has no noble antecedents. My father's money results from calloused hands and years of building up small workshops into big factories. That's allowed him to run the stables.'

'All the more credit to him and to your forebears. I'm not afraid of hard work, Annabel. Nor can I help being born into a family having an endless line of gloomy male portraits lining the walls of the ancestral home.' He loved seeing her smile. 'I take my turn with the lambing and the harvests, like the estate workers do. I muck out the stables whenever I have the time.'

Her eyes widened. 'I never knew that.'

'With respect, you know very little about me. I'm no Champagne Charlie. Not like Lucinda's chum, the aptly named Charlie Bell. I mean no disrespect towards any acquaintance of your family, but that gentleman and my former fiancée are soulmates. Except maybe for the minor detail of his having no title to lay at her dainty hooves.'

Annabel giggled. 'And I'm no Champagne Charlotte, either. I much prefer horses to people.' She held his gaze. 'But I think I'd enjoy dancing with you. Especially if it were something lively.'

'I'd better warn you in advance that the Charleston defeats me. But you must have many beaux queuing up in hopes of finding favour. I'm well aware you're regarded as one of the most admired debutantes of last year's group.'

'Is that what you've heard? What rubbish. How would anyone know what I'm really like? All those balls and parties and fussing and flirting — mere froth, in my opinion.'

Lawrence had to restrain himself from going on bended knee and proposing. He mustn't rush her, even if he rejoiced at discovering such a precious gem. But he fully intended to woo her, whether dining at London's Savoy Grill or in Somerset, kneeling on straw in his father's lambing shed. She had looked rather splendid in her jodhpurs when they first met on Christmas Eve.

He couldn't resist taking her hand in his. 'Your parents made me welcome at a time when I wished to spare my own family embarrassment. Maybe you'll at least accept my invitation to luncheon sometime soon? Not until after you return to full health, of course.'

Her gaze dropped to their joined hands. 'That would be very nice indeed.' She looked up again. 'Depending upon the weather in the New Year, don't you think?'

'I'll need to return to my office before too much longer, but please leave the arrangements to me, Annabel. I enjoy arranging surprises, even if I do possess a pea-like brain!'

'Why do you say that?'

He stood up, walked over to pluck a mistletoe sprig from a garland on the mantel shelf, and moved near her again. 'Because I've almost wasted an opportunity.'

He held the mistletoe above her

head, took a deep breath, and kissed her cheek. She said nothing. Heartened, he kissed her lips.

Swiftly she moved away.

'Are you angry?' he asked her.

'No, Lawrence. But my mother has realised we're alone, so we'd better be prepared for her to come over and coo. I suspect you must meet many mothers hoping to make a good impression.'

He hid the mistletoe behind his back. His lips twitched. 'Not for a while, actually. But I understand what you're saying. Lily has already impressed me, but not, of course, as much as her daughter has.'

★ ★ ★

Over a leisurely breakfast the next morning, Lawrence asked Annabel if she'd like him to ride Juno.

'Oh, I so wish I could ride her myself.'

Mr Crawford rustled his newspaper and peered over the top. 'You know that's impossible, my dear. You should be grateful Lawrence is kind enough to offer when the lads are busy preparing my horses.'

'I am grateful, Pa. Thank you, Lawrence.'

Lawrence winked at her once her father retreated behind his copy of *The Times*. 'Think how appreciative Great Aunt Hester is for all that reading aloud you've done.'

She inclined her head. This wasn't going to be easy, but one of them must be brutal for both their sakes. She'd spent most of the previous night tossing and turning.

He smiled at her across the table. She melted, and told her stupid heart not to beat so fast when she was trying to be ladylike and calm. And how about sensible? Hadn't she prepared this plan during her troubled night? It was ridiculous to feel so happy in Lawrence's company, yet so desolate to think of him leaving the next day for London. She told herself he'd volunteered a vague luncheon invitation out of politeness and to make amends for his valet taking her name in vain. Soon he'd be on his way in his shiny red Bentley. She'd known this man a matter of days, out of which she'd spent most of the time disapproving of him. So why did she feel so bereft when she knew her crush on Lawrence must never go further?

She barely responded when her mother arrived. Lawrence chatted with Lily Crawford while Annabel wondered which top-drawer debutante prowling London's salons and restaurants would be the lucky girl to win his heart. He was unlikely to remain single long, especially when Lady Lucinda's duplicity became known. He'd surely be deluged with invitations and awash with sympathy and apologies. He'd soon forget the gauche young daughter of the wealthy businessman who helped him out of a scrape.

'Penny for your thoughts,' he said, smiling at her.

'I'm sorry. I thought you were still talking to my mother.'

'She's gone to read her mail. Your father's heading for the stables, which is where I'm off soon.' His blue eyes spilled concern. 'I'm delighted your parents are content to leave us alone together, but you seem so far away; so troubled. I hate seeing you like this.'

She didn't know what to say, and focused her gaze on an oil painting of her father's favourite racehorse. How could she possibly convince Lawrence that despite last night's fireside chat, their budding romance could never blossom?

'I thought we were friends, Annabel. Last night I so enjoyed our conversation. I thought you enjoyed my company too. Please tell me why you seem so distant. Do you regret our kiss beneath the mistletoe?'

She felt tears sting. Angrily, she shook her head. 'I'm trying to be realistic about you and me, Lawrence.'

'Whatever do you mean? Actually, I've decided it best to return to London this afternoon, but it's not as if I'm sailing for America.'

The truth is, you can't wait to get away she thought. *That's just as well, because it's far too soon for you to begin a friendship with another silly girl.*

'Will you permit me to leave my address and telephone number? I already have yours, of course. Annabel, please answer me.'

Still the right words refused to come. She'd lain awake the night before, going over their fireside conversation. When he mentioned seeing her again, she'd been flattered. Intrigued. Excited. Not long later, she'd woken from an uneasy sleep, doubt poking inside her head like an icy, probing finger. Now she couldn't even excuse herself from the table and escape upstairs because of her stupid, stupid ankle.

'Do you still wish me to exercise Juno?' Lawrence asked. 'Shall I go to the stables now? Will I see you at luncheon?'

'Yes, of course. Thank you. Whenever it's convenient. But I'm not sure I'll feel well enough to come to luncheon, Lawrence. Please forgive me, but I'm

112

really not myself this morning.'

'Let me summon Bassett to help you to your room.'

'I'm sure I can manage.'

The perceptive Mr Bassett would suspect something, and the last thing she wanted was to burst into tears. But for her father's money, she could well be working alongside the valet as a parlour maid in some big house, or as a governess if she'd managed to get herself enough learning. Norman might be able to vanquish scheming society girls, but he couldn't smash down class barriers. Without blue blood running in her veins, she'd been a fool even to dream of a future with the young viscount. She shrank from the thought of what his parents would say about such a union. But that could never take place, so why risk heartache by pretending otherwise?

'Thank you, Lawrence, but I think I shall sit here a little longer on my own.'

'Well, that's told me, hasn't it? All right, Annabel. Whatever you think best. If I've offended you in any way, please accept my sincere apologies.'

He left the room without saying another word. Without even the hint of a backward glance.

Annabel put her head in her hands. If he was upset it could only be hurt pride. But her feelings for Lawrence, so unexpectedly kindled on Christmas Eve, would not, she knew, be easily extinguished.

★ ★ ★

Juno, with Lawrence in the saddle, cantered from the stable yard and down the drive. The lad called Tommy had recommended crossing over the road and following a bridle path with superb views.

Lawrence, once in the saddle and grasping the reins, felt his tension ease. How stupid he'd been. Annabel was too young and newly fledged in society to realise how, with her intelligence, wit and beauty, she'd make most upper-class young women of his acquaintance seem like dolls.

Despite learning how Lucinda had wronged him, Annabel was bound to have doubts over a friendship with him. If only she knew his true feelings. If only she knew she need feel no reticence about her background, if indeed that was her concern. His former fiancée always boasted about her royal connections, but she'd proved her morals were questionable. He knew very little about Miss Annabel Crawford, but he knew which one he'd trust.

For sure, women were strange creatures, and he still couldn't understand what had happened between last night and this morning to return Annabel to the same frigid civility he experienced after he introduced himself on Christmas Eve. But there was no point in trying to coax her into a more cordial state of mind. He had business to attend to in London and it really wouldn't wait much longer. He also needed to visit his parents and explain to them why their only son appeared to have behaved in such a cavalier fashion.

He and Juno were wandering now over woodland tracks. Beyond the trees he saw a stretch of water gleaming in the feeble sunshine. He'd take a turn around the lake before heading back. After luncheon, he and Bassett would say their goodbyes and leave for London. The Christmas interlude ended here.

★ ★ ★

'His lordship wants to set off after luncheon,' Norman explained to Phyllis, 'but I can't finish packing until he returns and gets changed.'

'You can eat with me soon as the desserts go into the dining room.'

He nodded. 'Thank you, my dear. I can complete the packing by then. But first I want to give you this.' He held out his hand. 'I've written down the addresses and telephone numbers of my London residence and the family seat.' He winked.

She clicked her tongue and tucked the envelope in her apron pocket. 'Thank you. I don't suppose you've seen Mr

Jeffers anywhere?'

'Not since breakfast. Shall I look for him?'

'It mightn't be a bad idea. The master might've asked him to tinker with the Rolls Royce, and Mr Jeffers has been known to lose track of time. We don't carry a big staff, as you know. It's important he gets his meal promptly, especially with Lord Lassiter here for luncheon.'

'Leave it with me, my dear.'

Norman Bassett was in no hurry to leave Starminster Manor. He enjoyed London and was partial to music halls and picture houses in his time off; but having been reunited with Phyllis, he didn't relish leaving her for the second time in their lives.

He was also anxious to gain his daughter's confidence. He'd had very little to do with Emmie over the festive period and didn't yet know how her mother intended to explain how she could suddenly afford to buy smart travel clothes, let alone pay for train tickets and accommodation.

But he had an errand to carry out. The Rolls Royce was kept beneath a lean-to at the far end of the stables. As soon as he glimpsed the car, Norman sucked in his breath and began to run, just as Tommy came into the yard — already reaching, Norman suspected, for the makings of a crafty smoke.

'Tommy! Come quick.'

'Where's the fire, Mr Bassett?' Tommy moved faster than Norman.

'It's Mr Jeffers. See?'

'Oh, blimey.' Tommy sprinted the remaining distance, skidding to a standstill beside the butler. He dropped to his knees. 'He's unconscious but breathing, Mr Bassett. He'll take some lifting, I fancy.'

Norman crouched beside the pair and tried to find a pulse. 'Mr Jeffers, can you hear me?'

'Cripes,' said Tommy as they waited for a response.

'How far away is the family doctor?'

'He lives in the village.'

'I'll stay with Mr Jeffers while you get

someone to phone. Come straight back and help me manhandle our friend onto the back seat of the Bentley, and I'll drive it round to the front door.'

'I'll shout for Will on the way. Three's better'n two.'

Bassett saw the butler's eyelids flicker open. 'Mr Jeffers?'

The butler groaned. 'My leg . . . I slipped on an oily patch. Fell awkwardly.'

'We're sending for the doctor. But we can't leave you on that stone floor. You'll freeze. Keep awake, man, do!' Bassett shrugged off his jacket and placed it over Mr Jeffers, who groaned but managed to whisper his thanks.

Bassett's quick thinking resulted in one very puzzled viscount as Lawrence, trotting back into the stable yard, caught a brief glimpse of his beloved Bentley, driven by his valet, pulling up at the front door. Despite his dejection, the young viscount, seeing only a bulky shape upon the car's back seat, couldn't fail to find humour in the situation. 'Crikey,' he said to Juno. 'What on earth's Bassett up to? For a moment I wondered if he was eloping with the cook.' He groaned. 'I wish your mistress would elope with me, Juno. But there's as much chance of that happening as there is of me travelling to the moon.'

Bassett got out of the car. 'I'm afraid Mr Jeffers has had a bad fall, my lord. We need to get him inside.'

Lawrence slid from the saddle as Tommy and Will arrived together. 'If one of you would kindly see to Juno, I can help with Mr Jeffers.'

'Thank you, sir. I think he's passed out again.'

'Let's hope the doctor arrives soon.' Lawrence exchanged glances with Bassett.

★　★　★

Annabel, unsure whether she dreaded or yearned for Lord Lassiter's imminent departure, arrived in the dining room, knowing her absence from luncheon would provoke unwelcome interest from her mother. She allowed her concentration to wander while everyone discussed the implications of Mr Jeffers being laid up with a broken leg in the cottage hospital. But then a remark from the young viscount penetrated her gloom.

'If I may make so bold, I've come up with a simple solution.' Lawrence rested his knife and fork. 'I intend to leave Bassett with you.'

'We can't possibly allow that,' said George Crawford.

'Oh yes you can. Bassett's well accustomed to acting as valet, butler, footman and chauffeur. He can probably stand on his head too. Rest assured, I'll manage until you make other arrangements.'

'Are you quite sure, my boy? It's an amazingly generous offer.'

'I'll never forget your kindness, taking a complete stranger in for the holiday. Besides, Bassett will probably enjoy a break from me. I have a cook who comes in when we're in town, or I can stay at my club if necessary.'

'Well, if you're quite sure, my boy. From what we know of him, I'm sure

Mr Bassett will be perfect.'

'Would you mind my enquiring whether he's happy to stay on, your lordship?' Annabel focussed her stern gaze upon Lawrence.

'Annabel, really!' Lily Crawford frowned at her daughter.

'That's all right, Lily.' Lawrence looked across at Annabel. 'I can assure you, Miss Crawford, that I've already consulted my valet and obtained his consent to the arrangement.'

Hearing that chilly 'Miss Crawford' hit Annabel like a snowball in her face.

Lawrence turned towards his host. 'As you know, I shall be bidding you farewell after luncheon. When you've secured another butler from the agency, Bassett can travel back to London by train and join me at my townhouse whenever he's satisfied it's convenient for him to leave.'

'We're most grateful, Lawrence.' George Crawford beamed at his guest. 'I'll come and see you off when you're ready. I must say, I think you're wise to get on the road. I think the snow every-one keeps talking about might actually reach us later today.'

Annabel's appetite had vanished. But who could blame Lawrence for wanting to escape? He seemed to have enjoyed the festivities, but he must still be questioning the return of her icy demeanour. If only he realised how she was putting up her defences only to shield herself from humiliation and heartache in future months. She needed to be cruel to be kind.

Somehow she got through the rest of the meal, excused herself from drinking coffee, and took refuge in her room where a coal fire welcomed her. Lawrence had risen and extended his hand in polite, frosty farewell. That had been hard to bear. She'd so nearly crumbled. So nearly begged him to stay.

Now she sat gazing at the wintry garden and berating herself for her stupidity. She saw a few snowflakes drift from the leaden sky but took no notice whatsoever, so intent was she on trying to analyse her recent behaviour and trying to persuade herself she'd acted for the best. The events of Christmas Eve and the following days had proved she lacked maturity and possessed about as much common sense as a cushion. She'd been wrong to condemn Lawrence for behaving badly without considering there might be another side to the scandal. Even after deciding to distance herself, she'd been pleased enough for him to ride Juno to hunt. Her cheeks burned as she recalled incidents and chance remarks, all of which must have convinced him of her stupidity and shallowness. Last night when they'd sat together chatting at the fireside, she'd felt happier than she had in ages.

But maybe the demons disturbing her night's sleep had arrived for a purpose. Maybe Lawrence would decide a bachelor's existence was the life for him, given his recent experiences. If it weren't for that bird spooking her horse and causing her to fall from the saddle, she'd never have met Lawrence while still unaware of his identity. He'd been a kind stranger who happened to drive along the road in time to help a lone female in distress. An image of the good-looking young man gazing down at her, blue eyes filled with concern while he grasped the filly's reins, entered her mind's eye. She wasn't sure how long she'd been sitting there when she heard sounds from outside.

Annabel got up and peered cautiously around the curtain to see Lawrence, wearing overcoat, woollen scarf, and yellow driving gloves, bidding farewell to her father while Norman gave a last buffing to the already shiny car headlamps.

Whether by fate or whether by intuition, she didn't know, but something made Lawrence look up just as she took in the full scene. Their gazes locked. A frisson of shock passed between them like an electric jolt. He barely acknowledged her, though when his valet opened the driver's door he gave her the ghost of a smile before he slid behind the wheel, leaving her miserable and wondering, alone in the room she'd slept in since she was a small child without a care in the world.

* * *

Norman hurried to the rear of the house and deposited his chamois leather and duster in the boot room. As George Crawford had requested, he was prepared to present himself in the master's study in the company of Mrs Petts.

The cook, riffling through recipes while she sat beside the kitchen range, looked up and gasped as he appeared. 'I thought you were leaving straight after luncheon, Norman?'

'I'd never have driven away without saying one last goodbye. In a nutshell, his lordship's left me behind to help you out while a replacement for Mr Jeffers is found. I've been asked to accompany you to the study to meet with Mr Crawford. I hope that's convenient, Phyllis.'

Her mouth became a wide 'Oh' of surprise. He thought how obedience must be ingrained in her soul as, without hesitation, she rose and untied her apron strings. But her fumbling fingers betrayed her nervousness, making him long to help her.

'I don't know what's going on, Norman, but if this is your idea of a joke, you'll never hear the end of it.'

He chuckled but caught his breath on seeing the expression in her eyes. There was pleasure there, mixed with concern. Without her apron, she looked as she had at the servants' Christmas meal — a neat, attractive woman resisting middle age with the aid of her sense of humour and trim figure. But he hated to think she might be worrying.

'Phyllis, love, we're not going to the gallows, you know. Your employer merely wants to explain the situation and make sure we're all rowing in the same direction, so to speak.'

She nodded. He daren't take her in his arms, although he longed to do so. 'It's not my place to say anything before Mr Crawford talks to you,' he said. 'I didn't engineer this, I promise you.'

'It's been a succession of shocks this Christmas. I — I don't mean to seem discourteous, Norman.'

'I caught you on the hop, that's all.'

For a moment he thought she would snuggle against his chest, but she broke away as a door banged and their daughter came rushing in from the scullery.

'Guess what! Will just got back from an errand. He says it's snowing in the village. And pitching already.' She spotted Norman. 'Oh dear, shouldn't you be driving back to London, Mr Bassett?'

'There's been a change of arrangements, Emmie. Your mother and I are on our way to speak with Mr Crawford. But I'm sorry there's snow around. I hope it won't affect his lordship's journey.'

'We mustn't keep the master waiting, Emmie.' Phyllis smoothed her hair. 'While I'm gone, have a look through the cupboards, please. I need to know if we've caster sugar and desiccated coconut left after all that sweetie-making. Could you make a list of what's in stock?'

Phyllis sailed through the door,

leaving Norman to smile apologetically at Emmie before following.

Mr Crawford opened his study door as soon as Norman tapped. 'Come in and sit down, both of you. Mrs Petts, you take the easy chair.'

She sat down on the chintz-covered seat and clasped her hands in her lap. 'Thank you, sir.'

George Crawford waited for his newest member of staff to be seated before moving behind his desk. 'Please don't look so stern, Mrs Petts. This is merely a chat to work out how best we can rub along while Mr Jeffers is out of action.'

Norman saw relief flood Phyllis' face and hid a grin. He'd be sure to tease her for not accepting his own reassurances.

'I imagine it'll be a while before we get our butler back again, sir,' Phyllis said.

'You're quite right, Mrs Petts. Too long for us to do without his very able services unaided, but I'm delighted Mr Bassett here has kindly offered to help us out.'

'But how will Lord Lassiter manage without him all that time?' she asked.

'Ah, well, come Monday morning I shall be in touch with a domestic agency with a view to engaging a temporary man. With luck, we shall only delay Mr Bassett a short time.'

'That's a pity! I was wondering if . . . I mean, that's good. Yes. Good that his lordship won't be inconvenienced.'

Norman Bassett stared at the tips of his shiny back shoes. Could she have been wondering if he'd be around longer? Even hoping he was wangling his way into the household? He longed to know. Such a reaction from the woman of his dreams could influence any decisions about his future. He willed himself to maintain his composure.

George Crawford nodded. 'Yes, indeed. We're fortunate to have the help of such an experienced employee.' He leaned forward and placed both hands palms down upon the desk. 'Everyone will need to be a little flexible. More than usual, I should say. And until the new fellow arrives, I'm relying on you two good people to, shall we say, run the show. How does that sound, eh? Do you think you can work together and bring the best out in the men?'

Phyllis piped up, 'And the women, sir, pardon me for saying.'

George Crawford looked at his cook and chuckled. 'My apologies, Mrs Petts. For a moment there, I must have imagined I was back in the army.'

★   ★   ★

Lawrence squinted through the windscreen. Wretched weather. He'd dismissed the sulky sky as heralding rain, and Bassett had put up the Bentley's hood ready for the journey. Lawrence had been surprised to find the road through Starminster already carpeted in white; and now, heading towards Wiltshire, he realised the car's windscreen wipers were struggling to withstand the onslaught of thick feathery crystals.

He hoped this was only a short, sharp storm and that further on, when he headed east, his journey would become easier. No other motorists were braving the elements. Should he turn around and return to the manor house; try again tomorrow? Lawrence felt sorely tempted. But could he cope with the inevitable reaction of Annabel? She'd made her feelings plain, and he still stung at the memory. He couldn't understand her dramatic change towards him.

Presumably, despite explaining the circumstances of his broken engagement — already hinted at by his loyal valet — Lawrence was still out in the cold. He smiled grimly, thinking how appropriate that description was at that moment. He was kitted out for arctic conditions, but the thought of progressing mile after mile, only to find a steep hill rearing ahead like some treacherous white-coated beast, filled him with frustration and no little unease.

He'd driven five miles or so. Ahead of him, the road sloped sharply downwards. Lawrence, feeling the car veer from side to side, steered towards the verge, slowing and completing his descent without hurtling too hastily through an onslaught of icy confetti. He managed to manoeuvre the Bentley until the car sat on the verge, tilting a little to port, but safely off the highway.

He switched off his engine. Now he faced the prospect of finding shelter. Already, heaped snowflakes partly obscured the windscreen. What a fiasco. He hadn't bargained for this. Nor could he recall how far the next signs of habitation were. Even then, unless he could find a hotel or police station or big estate, he didn't think much of his chances. He stared into whiteness and wondered how he could have been so stupid as to set off, especially alone, mainly because of a girl.

★　★　★

Bassett peered through the kitchen window. 'It's settling with a vengeance. I wish I knew whether it was only local or not.'

'You're thinking of his lordship?' Phyllis said.

'Of course.'

'Maybe he's stopped somewhere. You know what the upper classes are like. He could be sitting in some little hotel, sipping mulled wine and snug as a bug in a rug.'

'I don't recall seeing any hotels on that stretch of road. By my reckoning, he can't have driven more than five or six miles.'

Phyllis frowned. 'The next village has an inn. It's probably six or seven miles from Starminster, down a steep hill. You wouldn't notice the inn from the main road.'

'If he's there, I hope his lordship will think to telephone and let us know he's all right. If he doesn't, it'll be a worry.'

Phyllis walked over to join him. He felt her fingers squeeze his hand. 'You should speak to Mr Crawford about your concerns. He's sure to telephone the inn and enquire. Or he could ring the police station at Starminster — wouldn't they know about road conditions?'

He turned to her. 'That's a good idea. I think I should try and do something,

Phyllis. There's nobody expecting him back in London. I wouldn't mind betting that if he hasn't found somewhere to shelter, he'll be feeling like a boat afloat on a strange sea with no lighthouse to guide him.'

'Then you must try and make sure he's safe.'

★ ★ ★

Annabel yawned and put down her book. She'd begun reading *The Age of Innocence* after her mother had given her a copy at Christmas. Love, duty, passion, plus the struggle to reach the right decision — all these things seemed so relevant. Not that she'd any decisions to make. The chance of finding love seemed far, far away, even after meeting someone who appealed to her and who'd behaved impeccably over the few days she'd known him. She didn't have the guile of his former fiancée, nor would she wish to act like the wealthy flappers who lived for the moment.

Now she'd fallen in love with Lawrence, she realised the futility of attending social events she viewed as nothing more than cattle markets. And the last thing she wanted was for her mother to insist he might still be a possible suitor. Alone in her room, while Lawrence drove away from her, mile upon mile, she wondered why she'd resorted to extreme chillness rather than friendly politeness. After all, the original plan was for him to stay a few nights in the country before returning to London. She was unlikely to encounter him unless fate caused their paths to cross, but she couldn't think how that might happen. Again, her impetuousness had taken over.

Annabel swung her legs so she sat on the edge of her bed. She looked down at her feet and gently prodded around her right ankle. It felt fine. The swelling had vanished. Maybe she could sneak out and give Juno some exercise. It would do both horse and rider good.

She stood, walked to the window, and caught her breath at the sight of a winter wonderland. While she was reading and half-dozing, lulled by the coal fire's warmth, snow had blanketed the ground, magicking trees and shrubs into white marble sculptures. But it had stopped now. She'd be fine. Juno wasn't afraid of snow and nor was Annabel. She walked across to the wardrobe and took out jodhpurs and a hacking jacket, elated at the thought of escaping the house.

As Annabel stole downstairs, she felt confident about climbing into the saddle again. For fear of bumping into either parent, she headed down the staff corridor, intending to slip through the door to the yard.

She walked into the kitchen to find Norman, dressed for the great outdoors and accepting a Thermos flask from Mrs Petts.

'My goodness, you two look very serious.'

'Miss Annabel, please pardon my impertinence, but you're surely not going out?' Norman said.

'I'm hoping to take a short ride. The

snow has stopped. My ankle is better. I don't see a problem, but I'm longing to know who that flask is for.'

She saw Mrs Petts bite her lip and watched a shadow cross Norman's usually serene countenance.

'You don't have to tell me,' said Annabel. 'It's really none of my business.'

'I've just spoken with your father and expressed my concerns about his lordship. I'm afraid he might be in trouble because of the snowstorm.'

Annabel felt as though her heart was being torn from her chest. She stared at Norman. 'But surely he left straight after luncheon?'

'Precisely, miss. He could have driven only a few miles when the snow's full impact became apparent. Your father has been in touch with the police, also with the first hostelry along the route his lordship was following.'

'With what result?'

'Nothing, Miss Annabel. I'm setting off now to see if he — if maybe he's pulled over and sheltering in the Bentley.'

'Setting off how?'

'Tommy's bringing the horse and cart round.' He gave a wry smile. 'It appears the old ways are sometimes the best, miss.'

'But I can go faster if I ride Juno. I can go ahead of you.'

'I can't allow that, miss. What on earth would Mr Crawford say?'

'Nothing. Because no one's going to tell him. Isn't that right, Mrs Petts?'

The cook met Annabel's gaze. 'Indeed it is, Miss Annabel. But please don't delay. Make the most of the daylight.'

Annabel nodded and headed for the door, opening it just as Tommy brought the pony and trap round. She smiled as she thought of how Norman had described this means of transport, making it sound like something a rag and bone man would travel in.

'I'm saddling up, Tommy. Hope to overtake you soon.'

'Cripes. Well done, Miss Annabel.'

She hurried towards the stables. At least someone thought she had the right idea. And Mrs Petts probably had an inkling of what Annabel was feeling. The cook had known her since she was a small girl.

Juno seemed glad to see her mistress. She whickered and tossed her mane as if saying it was time for fun. Will, hurrying to check what was happening, helped Annabel prepare her horse and, finally, to provide a leg up into the saddle.

She smiled down at him. 'Thank you. Wish us luck, Will.'

'All the luck in the world, miss. I'll be waiting for you when you come back with his lordship.'

* * *

Lawrence, huddled beneath the tartan rug Bassett always kept upon the Bentley's back seat, cursed himself for setting off in such a nonchalant manner. Why hadn't he used his wits and left after breakfast? Annabel's attitude had been painfully clear by then. He could have been safe at home, warm and comfortable, instead of trapped in his car, for whose shelter he was of course grateful. But he hated feeling so vulnerable; so reliant on help that might or might not materialise.

But if he'd left, he wouldn't have been there when Jeffers fell. He wouldn't have been there to offer the services of Norman Bassett. And how beautiful the countryside looked in white, with the daylight bouncing off the dazzling landscape. Maybe if he walked a little further, he might come across a farmhouse.

He wondered whether anyone was thinking about him. His parents must still believe he'd besmirched his reputation and assume he was holed up with friends. Well, he was certainly falling into plenty of potholes in the course of returning to a life without Lucinda. His heart hadn't been broken as easily as his engagement. But if this feeling of dangling in mid-air meant what he suspected it meant, he'd be living with this awful bruised sensation for who knew how long. It served him jolly well right for allowing the delicious Annabel

Crawford to delude him.

Yet, had she? At the tender age of nineteen she was far too young for him, of course. What did she know of romance and passion? Come to think of it, what did he, at the age of 25, know about either of those matters? But how did one learn to play the game, if one didn't allow one's emotions to throw the dice?

He looked at his watch and grimaced. Another couple of hours and daylight would dissolve into dusk. The temperature would fall even lower. He must make a decision and make it fast.

★   ★   ★

Annabel overtook the pony and trap about three miles along the road. She waved as she trotted by, hoping Juno wouldn't want to stop for a chat. But all seemed well with the Irish mare. Luckily the sky had lost its ominous look, and Annabel thanked her lucky stars for the good visibility helping her along the snowy ground.

It wasn't long before she spotted

Lawrence's Bentley at the bottom of the hill. She patted Juno's neck and leaned in to whisper a warning, slowing the mare to a sedate walk down the verge towards the abandoned car. She reached the bottom of the slope but saw no sign of the driver. He must have got out and done his best to clear the windows and running boards. Annabel sucked in her breath and prepared to dismount.

Clutching Juno's bridle, snow crunching beneath her boots, she walked round to the driver's side and tried the door handle. It opened at once. She checked both seats in case Lawrence had scribbled a note saying where he'd gone. She'd seen no sign of any other vehicle having attempted the road, so knew he must have gone to find help or was sheltering somewhere nearby.

Now she was in a quandary. Should she wait for the others, or should she follow the footprints marking which way he'd set off? She decided that Norman and Tommy would know she'd gone ahead; and if she didn't, she might just as well have stayed at home, reading by the fire.

She scrambled back into the saddle and urged the filly on. They'd covered only a few yards when she spotted a distant figure. Her stomach lurched. Could that really be Lawrence walking so slowly, head down, his whole posture suggesting despair?

He still didn't look up, probably because he hadn't heard them approach along the snow-covered grass verge. Annabel called to him, her voice ringing through air cold and crisp as a crunchy apple.

He halted and looked up. 'Miss Crawford — is that beautiful apparition really you?'

'Of course it's me! But for goodness sake, call me Annabel.'

He laughed aloud and hastened towards her. 'Yes, all right, Annabel. I'll call you anything you wish. You must know how delighted I am to see you — but surely you're not riding alone?'

He stood alongside Juno, looking up. She saw the concern in his expression and told herself not to dismount and enter the shelter of his arms. This wasn't the time for personal discussions. Time was far too precious to waste when they were miles from home with the daylight fading away.

'Norman and Tommy are behind me in the pony and trap,' she said. 'You must be frozen.'

'More cross than frozen. Look at the trouble I've caused!'

'We must keep moving, unless you think we should wait in the Bentley. Norman and Tommy have shovels and sacks, so they might be able to dig the car out.'

'I'm not sure if she'll get up that hill, though I could follow the tyre tracks I left coming down. That wasn't much fun, but I reached the bottom without damage.'

'We have to decide what to do.' Annabel shifted in the saddle and grimaced. Her ankle had probably had enough for one day, though she wouldn't admit it.

But Lawrence noticed. 'You are an amazing, brave girl, coming to find me. But I'm worried your ankle won't take much more exercise.'

'Don't worry about me. When the

others arrive, we can sort something out.'

'I'm hoping that if we can get the car moving again, Bassett can drive you home and I can ride back before nightfall.'

They approached the abandoned vehicle. Annabel peered at the road sloping upwards, but the only movement she saw came from a flock of starlings hastening home to roost. They soared and dipped in the sky like a black shawl whipped by the wind.

'How far behind are the chaps, do you think?' Lawrence asked.

She shrugged. 'Not more than a few minutes.'

'Why don't you sit inside while I keep Juno company?'

'I'm wondering whether we should start for home. What if something's happened to them, Lawrence? A problem with the pony, or a broken axle?'

'I have a torch in the Bentley and a rug. You make a good point.'

'But you should lock the car.'

'All I care about is getting you home safe and sound and for Norman and

Tommy not to be in some sort of pickle. I'm concerned that if something's happened, it'll mean a long walk back for us all. And you should definitely rest that ankle.'

'All right. Let's wait a few more minutes.'

He opened the rear door as she slid from the saddle. 'I've got Juno. Put your feet up and tuck that rug around you.'

'I'll wind down the window so you can hear what I have to say.'

He shook his head. 'You don't need to say anything.'

'I think I do. I've behaved appallingly and I want to apologise for my rudeness. Most of all for my stupidity.'

Lawrence smiled as Juno dipped her head as if trying to listen too. 'I'm not sure if she agrees with you or not.'

'I wish you'd take me seriously, Lawrence. I'm not a schoolgirl anymore.'

'I know that. But you're young and beautiful, and I understand how you must have felt about having to spend the festive period helping to entertain someone whose reputation seemed, shall we say, sullied.'

'When you brought my horse to me after my fall, I thought you were the nicest young man I'd met in ages.'

'And I thought you were utterly delightful. I'd no idea who you were, but I wanted to get to know you better.'

'Then you introduced yourself and I allowed my stupid perceptions to distance me from you. I can't believe how childishly I behaved.'

'I understood why you were so chilly, but it hurt like blazes.'

Annabel sighed deeply. 'I've been very stupid. Twice.'

'Not half as stupid as I've been over you-know-who.'

She smiled. 'I've seen photographs of her in the society magazines. Was she truly that beautiful? In real life, I mean.'

'I used to think so. It's taken a while, but I know now what real beauty is.'

'Like Juno, you mean?'

'Um, I really meant, like Juno's mistress.'

Annabel laughed. 'I wasn't fishing for a compliment!'

'I know. That's why you're so refreshing. And now you're blushing just a little, and you look more beautiful than ever. I keep telling myself I'm the last man you need — someone who everyone sees as a bounder.'

'But don't you see?' Annabel said eagerly. 'After Norman dropped hints about how gentlemanly you'd been towards Lady Lucinda, I began looking at you like I looked at that unknown young man who rescued me on Christmas Eve.'

'So what happened between Boxing Night and this morning, Annabel?'

'I woke in the small hours and couldn't stop trembling, wondering how I could possibly think for one moment you'd be interested in someone like me.'

Lawrence's gaze melted her insides. 'But you're not any old someone — you're Annabel. You already know I think you're beautiful and funny and brave.'

'And the daughter of a nouveau riche family,' she spoke quietly.

He hesitated. 'Ah. Now I understand. Would you believe it if I told you I couldn't care even one hoot about your money or ancestry?'

'In the latter's case, the absence of it,' she muttered.

'Some of my ancestors were blackguards, Annabel. How does that make you feel? Fisticuffs, forgeries, and financial fiascos ran rife until my great-great-grandfather broke the mould and restored some semblance of respectability to my family.'

She tilted her face upwards, afraid tears weren't far away but unable to resist.

Gently he nudged the Irish filly, making her shift enough for him to get closer to the open window. He stooped, edging forward until his lips were a heartbeat away from Annabel's.

'Hey! Is everything all right, my lord? Thank goodness we've found you.'

Lawrence sighed. 'The cavalry's here, Annabel. Your reputation is safe.'

* * *

Mrs Petts ladled hot chicken soup into a bowl and carried it across to Norman.

Annabel's father had insisted a bottle of wine should be opened.

'Thank you, Phyllis. This is most welcome, I can tell you. Is Tommy not joining us?'

'He tucked into his supper while you were all in with the master. Gone back out to join the others.'

'I couldn't have done without his help today.'

'He's a good boy.' She hesitated. 'I know I shouldn't ask, but I hope Miss Annabel didn't get a scolding.'

'Between you and me, his lordship saw to that. He couldn't praise her highly enough.'

Phyllis nodded. 'So what happened after you found them?' She pulled out a chair.

'Won't you take a drink with me? Mr Crawford keeps a good cellar.'

She smiled. 'I know. And I'll take a small glass to keep you company, Norman. I was too anxious to eat earlier, but I'll have something in a while.'

'Circumstances were worrying. When we came upon the scene, his lordship said they'd been trying to decide what action to take. Miss Annabel's ankle was troubling her and he wondered if they should start climbing that confounded hill and hope to find us.'

'They wouldn't have known about that track Tommy took, to cut out having to tackle the hill.'

'The lad said it was safer than chancing our luck on that treacherous slope.'

'I suppose his lordship and Miss Annabel could always have huddled up together in the back of the car for warmth.'

'What, horse and all?'

She giggled. 'I suppose they'd have had a problem squeezing Juno in. I reckon it's a good job you and Tommy arrived when you did. I fancy his lordship was relieved not to abandon that beautiful car of his.'

Norman nodded. 'I know I can say this without it going any further. I have the feeling something's been kindled between a certain two persons.'

She gulped her wine. Coughed. Fumbled for a handkerchief. He got to his feet and rushed round to pat her on the back. 'My word, I'm sorry if I shocked you.'

'Please don't interrupt your supper. I'm still breathing. It's just that I thought the same thing myself, as soon as Miss Annabel decided she was going to help find his lordship.'

Norman placed his hands on her shoulders. 'Can I — might I hope for something to have kindled between you and me, Phyllis?'

She twisted round to face him. 'Surely you can tell it has, Norman? Unless it never really went away in the first place?'

⋆   ⋆   ⋆

Lawrence and Annabel ate dinner with the footman attending upon them. Mr and Mrs Crawford were taking coffee in the drawing room. Lawrence waited until the young footman left the room after serving apple pie and custard.

'Who'd have thought I'd be back

again, having set off all those hours ago. I still feel embarrassed about causing such trouble.' He sighed. 'My father will probably disown me a second time.'

'Once he knows the full story, I think he'll be very proud of you,' Annabel said with a smile.

'One can only hope.'

'I don't even know if you have brothers and sisters.'

'One sister, married and living in Cheshire.'

'Younger or older than you?'

'Older by several years. I must've been an afterthought.'

'Your parents would have been thrilled to have a son and heir. I can't imagine you being disowned over a silly misunderstanding.'

He shrugged.

'Anyway, who did your sister marry?' She held her breath.

'A dreadful bounder. Caroline became the Duchess of Bailford.'

Annabel put down her spoon. 'You see? I was right.'

'What about?'

'About not being good enough for your family.'

'What rubbish. With respect, of course.'

She felt a pang for what she knew she couldn't have. 'Lawrence, you know very well I can't compete with upper-class girls like your sister.'

He leaned forward. 'There is no competition. It wouldn't be right to propose, but I want to ask your father's permission to court you, or woo you, or whatever the correct expression is. With your consent, of course, Annabel.'

'We hardly know each other.'

'That's what he'll say too, but we can soon change that. I have a plan, but I need to know how you feel about me. I realise you and your parents must consider me unsuitable in many ways.'

She sighed. 'You know that's not true. I wish I could make you understand how scandalised your family and friends would be to think of you choosing me as a prospective bride.'

'I shall treat that remark with the

contempt it deserves. They can't fail to adore you, except I don't want anyone else falling in love with you except me. And Bassett, if you know what I mean.'

'You're so funny, Lawrence.'

'Thank you. Does that mean I stand a chance?'

'You truly think your parents would approve?'

'Of course. They never really liked you-know-who, but understandably they were upset to think of me ditching the girl I was engaged to.'

'You must tell them the truth soon.'

'I fully intend to.'

'May I ask you something?'

'Ask away.'

'Might I have a private conversation with Norman tomorrow, please?'

'You're after knowing all my appalling habits?'

'No, but I'd like to ask him certain questions.'

'Good lord. Well, he does know me better than anyone, I suppose.'

'That's not the point. He told me

some of the places he worked before you employed him. I want to ask him things you mightn't think about.'

'Does that mean he'll be like some kind of marriage broker?'

Annabel laughed. 'Not at all. But I believe he'll give an honest appraisal of how I might be perceived in the circles you move in.'

'Right. So if he provides an answer you approve of, you'll say yes to me regarding an appropriate period of courtship?'

She turned her head. 'The footman's on his way. I'd know that tread anywhere.'

'I feel like someone in an espionage novel.' Lawrence leaned across the table and whispered, 'I'm desperate to know your answer. My next question will have to be in code.'

She tried to keep her laughter from bubbling up as the servant entered the room.

'This dessert is delicious. Do you agree, Annabel?'

'Yes, Lawrence, I do.' She took another

mouthful of apple pie and wondered whether the footman would think they'd both completely lost their reason.

★   ★   ★

'Excuse me, Miss Annabel. His lordship tells me you'd like a word.'

She looked up from the letter she was reading. 'Hello, Norman. Do sit down. My mother's breakfasting in bed today, so I'm borrowing her sitting room.'

'I trust Mrs Crawford is not indisposed, miss.' He seated himself on the nearest chair.

'She's had several late nights. That's all it is. Now, I expect you're wondering what all this is about.'

He inclined his head. 'I can't help noticing how his lordship keeps singing a certain popular song. I believe it begins with, um, 'It had to be you.''

'Goodness. Norman, I do believe you're on the right track.'

'I'm very happy to hear it, Miss Annabel.'

She nodded. 'I'm very happy too. I think you know that.'

'I do, miss, although I sense a 'but' coming.'

'Norman, how can I possibly allow Lawrence to court me when I have no title, no noble background?'

'With respect, Miss Annabel, that's absolute piffle.'

'Really? I get the distinct impression his parents are rather, well, sticklers for tradition. As for his sister, she's married to a duke, isn't she?'

'Between you and me, Caroline was a tearaway. She drove her parents to distraction. Broke hearts galore until she met the duke, and then . . . oh my word, I'm not sure I know how to put this.'

'Surely not a scandal?'

'A scandal in the making, miss. Suffice it to say the marriage took place with a minimum of fuss, and I'm delighted to say it would appear the couple are extremely happy together with their young daughter.'

Annabel sat back. 'I see. So that's

why Lawrence's parents gave him a hard time when they thought he'd jilted you-know-who. They feared more scandal.'

'Precisely. His lordship isn't always adept at defending his own actions. He is immensely polite and thoughtful of others.'

'And funny.'

'Indeed.'

'But I doubt his parents would find anything humorous in being asked to welcome little miss nouveau riche to their world.'

'I'll tell you something, Miss Annabel. You'll be like a breath of fresh air. And more importantly, you're worth ten of those flibbertigibbets who flatter themselves they're good enough to attract his lordship merely because a drop of blue blood runs in their veins.'

'Norman, I think I love you.'

'The feeling's entirely mutual, miss.'

They beamed at one another.

'Now, may I tell you my own secret?' he said.

'Of course, Norman. My lips are sealed.'

'I've popped the question to Phyllis Petts and she's said yes.'

Annabel blinked hard. 'You want to marry the lovely lady who is our cook?'

'Very much, miss.'

'But you've only known her since Christmas Eve.'

'With respect, Miss Annabel, my Phyllis and I have, shall we say, history. We first met more than seventeen years ago. In fact if you look at young Emmie, she's the living proof of our relationship.'

Annabel blinked hard again. 'Gosh. I won't ask anything further, but that really is quite some secret, Norman.'

'It is, isn't it? I'm not sure how all this will work out, but I'm determined not to give Phyllis up, not now I've found her again after all these years.'

'No indeed. Nor should anyone expect you to. I suppose this proves the best things are worth waiting for, don't you think?'

★   ★   ★

'You must wait to see in the New Year in with us, my boy,' George Crawford said to Lawrence. 'Apart from the fact that we enjoy your company, the roads won't be safe until then, if the weather forecast's anything to go by.' He smiled at Norman. 'Thank you so much, Mr Bassett. If you leave us that decanter, I think his lordship and I can manage quite well for the rest of the evening. I'm sure you'll appreciate an early night.'

'Thank you, sir. A very good night to you both.' Norman left the room quietly.

'Nice chap, that valet of yours. Extremely competent.'

Lawrence smiled fondly. 'He is indeed.'

George cradled his brandy goblet. 'You said you wanted to discuss something. Does it concern Bassett? I'll understand if you've had second thoughts about leaving him with us.'

'No second thoughts. What I have to say concerns your daughter.'

'Look, my boy, if you're thinking you need to buy some little trinket because she rode to your rescue, you really don't need to bother. Annabel's an impetuous girl. She relishes a challenge.'

'She's also brave and delightful to spend time with. A good horsewoman too.'

'You might add stubborn. Plus, she drives her mother crazy.'

Lawrence smiled. He stopped gazing at the logs burning brightly in the hearth. 'What I have to say may come as a surprise, Mr Crawford.'

'It's George, my boy.'

'Sorry. Here we go, then. George, I would like your kind permission to request Annabel's hand in marriage — only after a suitable time of courtship, of course, and without making a grand fuss and kafuffle, given events in my recent past.'

'Good grief.'

Lawrence gulped at his brandy. Fortunately it went down the right way. 'Thank you for being so understanding about that whole wretched business, George; for inviting me here for Christmas, and well, everything. It goes without saying that I didn't intend to fall in love when I turned up on Christmas Eve.'

'No, I don't expect you did.' George leaned forward. 'Do I take it my daughter is agreeable to this, er, courtship?'

'To my utter delight, yes, she is.'

'Good grief.'

'I have to say your daughter was not without some apprehension. I believe she might have found the whole thing about my ancestry rather daunting at first. I can't blame her for that — I'd be put off by that succession of reprobates too.'

'You might find it best not to repeat that opinion when speaking to my dear wife.'

'Understood.'

'But Lawrence, can we be absolutely clear about this? You wish to become engaged to Annabel after knowing her only a matter of days.'

'Not formally engaged, George. I don't want to risk putting her off the idea by rushing matters. I have certain duties to complete in London, after which I'd like your permission to come and take Annabel out for luncheon. Maybe present her with a little keepsake, as a token of my affection. Not a ring just yet, but some other item of jewellery.' He bit his lip and willed George Crawford not to say 'good grief' again.

'Great Scott.'

'I apologise if I'm speaking out of turn. I suspected my request would come as a shock.'

'It's just that my daughter has always maintained that being married isn't the be-all and end-all. She can be rather scathing about some of the young men she meets.'

Lawrence nodded. 'Annabel has made her opinions abundantly clear. I find her so very refreshing. Different, and funny. I feel I've discovered my soulmate, and fortunately it seems she feels the same about me. I hope so, anyway.'

'Great Scott.'

Lawrence struggled to swallow his mirth. 'I'm sorry to have sprung this on you after such a short acquaintance-ship, and with my former engagement so recent. Though I have to say, my feelings for your daughter are entirely different from those I experienced for the, um, other young lady.'

'Ah, but how am I, and indeed Annabel, to be sure of that?'

At once Lawrence panicked. He was making a botch of things. He took a deep breath. 'It's understandable you should be suspicious, George. I'm well aware Annabel is only nineteen while I'm several years older.'

'Which in itself isn't a problem,' said George. 'Had you known her for longer, I would be more understanding. But after meeting her less than a week ago, you're contemplating a future with her, something which until recently you were presumably planning with your former fiancée.'

This didn't bode well. Lawrence lifted his chin. 'What can I do to make you change your mind?'

'Give yourself time, my boy. I took a liking to you right from the first, and I understand the Lady Lucinda led you a fine dance. But Annabel is barely out of finishing school. She should meet more young men than she already has. It concerns me how she's formerly pronounced most of them as numbskulls, but out of the blue she's contemplating matrimony with you.'

'But I can't bear the thought of losing her.'

'If her feelings for you are as strong as you believe, surely that won't be an option? If I were you, I'd keep quiet about this. See how you both feel after a period of absence. You sound as though you're going to be busy in London as well as on your family's estate, so why not enjoy these extra few days with us and come back nearer the spring? Letters and telephone calls will help keep you both in touch.'

Lawrence nodded and even managed a ghost of a smile. But what did he expect? Any father worth his salt would be protective of his beautiful young daughter, even when a prospective suitor with a respected title appeared on the scene. In his turn, Lawrence respected George Crawford. But the thought of Annabel attending parties and dances around the county while the man who loved her kept a low profile filled him with dismay.

'I think that as soon as the road is passable, I shall be on my way,' he said. 'Spending Christmas with you has been most enjoyable, but I need to get on with my life now. Build some bridges. And hope, when the times comes, you'll feel confident I'm the right man to become Annabel's husband.'

★   ★   ★

'I can't believe you let me sleep in! Surely Lawrence didn't need to set off so early? Stupid, stupid weather.' Annabel sank into a chair and glared at the toast rack.

'The thaw set in last night,' said her father. 'He really does need to return to London.'

'But things have changed since yesterday. He's told you how we feel about each other, hasn't he?'

'He has indeed. I believe our discussion was perfectly open and honest.'

'You sent him away, didn't you?'

'On the contrary, Annabel. I suggested he stay over Hogmanay so the two of you could spend more time in each other's company.'

She stared at him, a cold hand squeezing her heart, draining her confidence. 'And he refused?'

'Annabel, believe me, I had only your best interests at heart when I suggested too much haste wasn't a good thing. I told Lawrence he could write and telephone. I got the feeling he decided it best to get back to everyday life. I'm sure you'll hear from him soon.'

'I can't believe you acted as you did.' She glared at her father. 'That dreadful woman will snap her jaws and get her teeth into him again.'

'If he allowed that to happen, after all he told me about his feelings for you, I would say you'd had a lucky escape, my dear. Your comment only serves to prove my point.'

'Which is?'

'That you may be nineteen years of age, but you're acting rather like a spoilt child. Have trust in the young man. Allow him to sort out his feelings and his relationship with his parents. Do you really want them to view their son's friendship with you as some sort of rebound liaison?'

Annabel frowned. 'I see what you mean. They might perceive me as someone totally different from the person I am; someone on the make.'

Her father chuckled. 'Good girl. Now, that remark shows me you're more than capable of behaving in a mature manner. Let's have some breakfast and discuss our plans for the New Year's racing schedule. You know how much I value your opinion.'

★   ★   ★

'We need to make plans, Phyllis.'

'There's been so much going on

round here, I'm not sure I can think straight, Norman. This is the first evening in weeks I'm cooking dinner for fewer than seven.'

He nodded. That was why he'd waited, anticipating her full attention. 'My word, these ginger biscuits are first-class.'

'Aren't they? And before you ask, yes, Emmie made them.'

'Which proves she has all the more reason to begin planning her new life.'

'She said you'd helped her make a list of hotels.'

'It's a good time of year to apply for a post, with the festivities behind us. Employees often change jobs once Christmas and New Year are over.'

'While I think of it, Mr Crawford says the agency are sending the new man at the weekend. Did you know?'

Norman gave her a wry smile. 'No. I'm not as important as you are.'

'Flatterer! More likely the master didn't want you buying your train ticket yet. He'll not want to let you go before he has to.'

'Perhaps. However, I know something you probably don't.'

She sat back in her chair and folded her arms. 'I'll need to put the joint to roast soon. Just marking your card.'

'I can take a hint. Lawrence plans to visit the weekend after next. So if all's well with Mr Jeffers' temporary replacement, I shall be returning to London in the Bentley.'

'I see.' Phyllis sighed. 'I suppose it could've been worse.'

'For us, or for poor Mr Jeffers?'

'At least we have a little more time together.'

'Phyllis, I know you won't like the idea, but for us to be together — as in married — you're going to have to leave Starminster Manor.'

She twisted the narrow gold band she still wore on her ring finger. 'I realise that, of course. I'll be sorry to go, but if Emmie leaves, there's nothing to keep me here, is there? Not when I can begin a new life with you.'

'Exactly. I can't wait. But I'd better

get on too. I just wanted to make sure we were singing from the same hymn book.' He rose. 'I might know more once I've spoken to his lordship about you and me. He may have something in mind.'

'You can't mean he'd take me on too?'

'I don't know. He might well be considering his own future, and he's made it clear he enjoys your cooking.'

'Has Miss Annabel said anything? About you-know-what?'

'All I can tell you is they're corresponding. She doesn't mention him when she asks me to post her latest epistle, but in my humble opinion she has a certain glow.'

'I can imagine those two making a lovely couple.'

'You've known her since she was a small child, haven't you?'

She nodded. 'Miss Annabel is two and a half years older than Emmie. She was six when I started here. She had a governess, and of course Emmie went to the village school. They played together at weekends. I've always had a soft spot for Miss Annabel, but Emmie never shared her love of horses.'

Norman nodded. 'That's bound to be a big consideration for Miss Annabel, in terms of whom she might marry and where she'd settle.'

'Because she'd rather stay in the country?'

'People have been known to keep horses in London.' He reached across and stroked her cheek. 'But we all know the young lady's views on people who exist on a diet of parties. It's fortunate his lordship feels the same.'

'Are you saying I should look to my wedding cake recipe?'

'Not for a while, I fancy. Emmie will be the one to move first, you mark my words.'

'You know I'll be pleased for her if — when that happens.' Phyllis' voice sounded wistful. Norman wished he could wave a magic wand to make everything slot into place.

'And you'll miss her very much. I'm not that daft. But when I talk about changes, I don't mean only for Emmie and us.'

Six months later

Annabel signed her name at the bottom of the page and screwed the top back on her pen.

Starminster Manor
14th June 1926

My darling Lawrence,
Thank you for your last letter, which arrived before I had time to answer the previous one. You're such a mystery man! I cannot think why I need to be collected by Norman and driven to my birthday luncheon, when Jeffers could have transported me. It's a pity I cannot drive myself, but I plan to learn, you know. It will be easier now Mr Jeffers has fully recovered, poor man. Did I tell you — he's lost weight, and it suits him! Mrs Petts has to hide goodies away

so he doesn't fall back into his former evil ways.

But to return to the matter at hand, I shall do as you request and make sure I'm ready for collection (like a parcel?) at ten o'clock on Friday morning. Also as requested, I won't wear anything too flimsy. On second thoughts, perhaps I should choose jodhpurs and hacking jacket?

My father is a hard taskmaster but I am enjoying everything I've taken on for him. We were away at Newmarket yesterday when Charlie Bell called to see me. Ma gave him tea on the terrace but she said he didn't hang around long. Apparently he asked whether I was spoken for. Isn't that frightful? Ma whispered to me that she thought Champagne Charlie's getting to the age where he could be my sugar daddy!

Perish the thought.

I'd better finish here if I want to catch the next post. It seems an absolute age since I last saw you, dearest Lawrence. Friday cannot arrive too

soon! Please tell Norman I look forward to a nice chat in the car.
With all my love,
Annabel

Once she'd read through her words, she added a couple of kisses and sealed the single sheet in a cream envelope, addressed to Lawrence at his London home.

Who'd have thought that months after their first meeting, she and he would still be continuing their friendship, even if conducted mostly by post. Her father had been wise, though at first she resented what she viewed as his quaint approach. Back in December she believed she'd never see Lawrence again, but he telephoned on reaching his house. He agreed her father's advice seemed harsh, but he felt they both needed time to adjust. Since then, he'd visited her every few weeks. On one occasion she travelled to London, where Norman Bassett met her train at Paddington Station and drove her to Lawrence's home. Lawrence's sister was

178

staying too, making Annabel feel delighted to be invited at the same time.

But she longed to see Lawrence more often. Annabel closed her eyes and imagined she was crossing a luxurious hotel foyer, her heels sinking into thick carpet as she walked towards him. He'd hold out his arms and whisper 'Happy birthday' while he held her close.

Annabel opened her eyes when she heard her mother call from the hallway: 'Annabel, are you going to join me for luncheon, or are you not? You know I have an appointment with my dress-maker at two thirty.'

She'd completely forgotten. But if she skipped lunch, she could hurry to the village and post her letter. Lovely Mrs Petts would see she didn't go hungry. She decided she wouldn't say anything about Norman collecting her on Friday, in case he arrived with no time left to visit his fiancée.

Her mother was calling again. Annabel picked up the letter and hurried from the room.

After a hilarious evening with his old school friend, Lawrence bid his host farewell and descended the elegant Regency house's front steps to find the chauffeur. The property, perched on the border between Wiltshire and Somerset, was the perfect place for a rendezvous, especially as Annabel would have no idea where Bassett would be taking her. All part of the plan.

His feet crunched on fine gravel as he headed for the stables. Lawrence lifted his hand in greeting when he saw the chauffeur crossing the yard and followed him to the vehicle waiting nearby. Five minutes later they were bumping along a rutted lane beyond which lay the field that Lawrence had come to know as well as his own toothbrush over the past several months. The chauffeur guided the car through the gate and stopped alongside the nearby hangar.

'There we are, my lord. I moved Dolly and parked her round the back.

She's fuelled up ready to roll. The rest's up to you.'

Lawrence laughed. 'Thank you, Mr Cannings. It is indeed up to me.' He checked his watch. 'They should be here any time now. Weather's looking good, don't you think?'

'It is, sir. I shall be back well before five, ready to assist. Maybe you'd like me to wait, rather than abandon you now?'

'That's very thoughtful of you, but I believe Mr Bassett won't be far away.'

'Whatever you say, sir.'

Lawrence waited until the chauffeur drove off before he approached the little aircraft. He walked all around, checking items he knew Mr Cannings had already inspected, wanting everything to be perfect for the most significant day of his life so far. He didn't have long to wait before hearing the purr of his Bentley's engine. Watching the car nose its way into the field, his heart beat a little faster.

'Lawrence, how dashing you look in

your leather jacket! Doesn't he look dashing, Norman?' Annabel exclaimed as she allowed the viscount to help her from the front seat. He knew it wouldn't have occurred to her to sit by herself at the back, and loved her for it.

He kissed her hand, wishing he could take her in his arms. 'Happy birthday, darling Annabel. You look amazing in those greens and blues. Like an elegant kingfisher!'

'I thought my culottes and tunic would fit the bill. But why are we meeting in a field? Norman refused to say one word about your luncheon plans. Not that I dislike picnics.'

Norman cleared his throat. 'I'll wait until you, erm, depart, shall I, my lord?'

'That would be good, Mr Bassett,' said Lawrence. 'Then you can drive back to Starminster and visit Mrs Petts.' He took Annabel by the hand. 'Come, Miss Crawford. Your carriage awaits.'

He watched her face as he led her round the hangar where the aircraft stood on the close-cropped turf.

'Lawrence, we're surely not going up! But where's the pilot?'

'Here beside you, my love. This is part of your birthday surprise.'

'I'm already speechless. How many other parts are there to my surprise?'

'Two. But let me help you on board.'

'What a good job I wore my culottes.' She climbed into the passenger seat.

'You'd have managed. But they're rather fetching. Did I already tell you that?'

'You didn't tell me you could pilot a plane. Is this really happening?'

'I've had an excellent instructor these past several months. I thought it would be a useful skill, and one that would amuse you, Annabel.'

She waited until she felt sure he was satisfied with the engine turning over, watching his every move as he prepared to taxi down the track.

'Where are we going?' she called above the rumble of the engine.

'Across the water. Don't worry, I'll try not to let your toes dip in the Bristol Channel.'

'Behave, Lawrence.' She felt no fear. All that mattered was that they were alone for once and having the perfect adventure.

'Hold tight. I'm about to get us airborne.'

He pulled back the stick. Annabel felt the thrust of the engine pin her to her seat as the frail craft raced along the runway. When that magic moment came and the wheels lifted the aircraft off the ground, she saw the tops of trees and the road winding like a ribbon below and laughed out loud.

Lawrence told her he was watching for his usual landmarks while keeping an eye on his instruments. 'It's not a long flight,' he said. 'We'll be eating an early lunch, so I hope you're peckish.'

'I'm still almost speechless.'

'Only almost? Just you wait, young lady.'

At that moment Annabel knew she loved him more than she'd realised it was possible to love a man. She decided that if he didn't ask her to marry him soon, she'd ask him herself.

'I can see an omnibus!' she shouted. 'It looks like a toy.'

'That farm to your right looks like the model one I was given when I was a little boy,' Lawrence said.

Annabel glued her nose to the window, enjoying a clear view of houses and railway tracks and church steeples. They crossed the Somerset coastline and she exclaimed at sight of a Victorian pier jutting away from a beach they both remembered visiting as children. They also agreed they weren't quite sure where the River Severn merged with the ocean, but they liked the way the sunshine turned the sea silver beneath their wings.

'There's just under nine miles between here and the Welsh coast,' Lawrence said.

'If we're landing on a beach, I hope it's not a pebbly one.'

'You'll be pleased to hear we'll be landing on ground owned by a friend of a friend. You'll be doubly pleased to hear I've flown there before.'

'Are we lunching with this friend of a friend?'

'Everything will be revealed after our arrival.'

Annabel knew better than to probe further. Her pilot obviously took lessons in discretion from Norman Bassett. She was enthralled with flying; captivated by this secret skill Lawrence had kept hidden.

*   *   *

'Norman Bassett! What on earth are you doing here?'

'Got a kiss for me? There's no one looking.' Norman closed the back door behind him, dumped his overnight bag at his feet, and held out his arms.

'Get away with you.' But Phyllis put down her whisk and hurried over.

'I've missed you so much, love,' he whispered, holding her.

'Same here. It's grand to see you. But I'm confused. Miss Annabel said you were collecting her first thing and driving her to meet his lordship. I assumed I wouldn't see you until you drove her back later.'

'It's a long story. Any chance of a cuppa?'

'Why don't you make us both one? The kettle's simmering, and I've sent Violet and the new girl out for a breath of fresh air.'

'I know how much you miss Emmie, but you must be pleased she's doing so well at the Strand.'

'Of course I miss her, but fair play — you and Mr Jeffers were right about her needing to move on. She loves her job, as you well know.' She glanced at the clock. 'There's a birthday dinner for Miss Annabel tonight. It's just a small party, but I want everything to be really special. The master and mistress are lunching out with friends, fortunately.'

'Sir Lawrence is, as I speak, romancing Miss Annabel.' Norman reached for cups and saucers.

'About time, too.' She frowned. 'You brought your bag in from the car. What's going on, Norman?'

'Poor Phyllis. Let me explain before

you beat me about the head with that rolling pin.'

She continued whisking batter for a sponge while she listened to his account of the morning's activities, raising her eyebrows when he mentioned the flight to Wales.

'I couldn't tell you anything because it was all hush-hush. Her father knows, of course.'

'She'll love it. Such a daredevil that girl is. But flying somewhere for lunch? The things these posh folk get up to.'

'His lordship may be top-drawer, but remember me saying to you he was a man of the people? A while back, I put my cards on the table and told him about you and me needing a position together.'

'Right.'

'It's taken all this time to bring his plans to fruition — his words, not mine — but this week he told me he wanted us to run his London house together for the foreseeable future, with some daily help of course. And, um, after we become man and wife, that goes without saying.'

'Are you serious?'

'Perfectly.'

'But what does his lordship mean by the foreseeable future?'

'Ah, now that's a bit trickier. Better brace yourself and think back to that night you and I sat here talking. That was after his lordship got himself stuck in the snow.'

'When you prophesied big changes for more people than just us?'

'Precisely. Please believe me when I say there's one more piece that needs fitting into the jigsaw.'

★   ★   ★

'Do you know what I was thinking, Lawrence, when you were flying us over the sea?'

'I'm hopeless at guessing. How's your sole meunière?'

She leaned towards him. 'Delicious. Everything's delicious. But what I was thinking was, if you hadn't driven into a snowstorm after Christmas when you were trying so hard to get away from me, today would never have happened. We'd have gone our separate ways.'

'It was fate taking a hand, Annabel. And I would point out that I never wanted to get away from you. I fell in love with you as soon as I saw you and your jodhpurs sitting in that ditch. You were the one who drove me away, my angel.'

'I know. And I'm so sorry. I was such a child.' She sighed.

'Have some more champagne and let's not talk about the past.'

'I adore champagne.'

'I know you do, but I'm not allowing you to get tiddly, Miss Crawford. Not today, anyway.'

She put down her knife and fork. 'Today's my twentieth birthday. Aren't I entitled to some tiddlyness? Another year and I shall be properly grown up and utterly boring.'

He chuckled. 'You could never be

boring. But I hope one or two things about you will have changed by the time next June arrives.' He reached inside his waistcoat pocket.

'Lawrence?' She gasped at sight of a small leather box.

'Annabel, will you do me the immense honour of becoming my wife?' He pushed his chair back and dropped on one knee, then opened the box and took out a ring. 'Crikey, was I supposed to say please?'

She gasped a second time. 'Lawrence, darling man — are you quite, quite sure about this?'

'I am, because I love you very much. Annabel?'

'I love you very much too. I'm as sure of my feelings as I am about letting you fly me to the moon if you wished.'

'Not sure Dolly could make it, but I love it that you trust me.' He slid the diamond ring upon Annabel's finger. 'The ring is the next part of the surprise. I must admit to a huge amount of relief that you've accepted me — apart

from the fact that I love you, I mean.'
He rose and smiled down at her.

'I'm not sure I understand.'

'All will be revealed. There's another couple you know about who love one another and who deserve to be together.'

She stared at him. 'You mean Norman and Mrs Petts, don't you?'

'That chap is always turning up, even when he's not here. Yes, I do mean those two, and I know how fond you are of them. Now, why don't we order a couple of portions of Eton mess or something equally jolly, before I whisk you back to England? There's more to come, my love. Believe me.'

'I adore Eton mess — but aren't you forgetting something?'

Lawrence stooped and kissed her tenderly, totally ignoring the giggles from nearby diners.

'There you are, my darling. I've plighted my troth.'

* ★ ★

192

'How lovely that the master invited us in to drink the happy couple's health,' Phyllis said. 'I must say, it seems strange to think of Miss Annabel becoming a viscountess.'

'I'm immensely relieved she is,' Norman said. 'I might've been forced to seek other employment if his lordship had married you-know-who.'

'We'd still have got together, but this way you and I can work for people we respect and care about.'

'Indeed. His lordship has given me permission to tell you one more thing, Phyllis, while you finish your champagne.'

'Is this the missing jigsaw piece, Norman?'

'It is. There was always the chance Miss Annabel would decide not to marry his lordship.'

'You'd never have let that happen.'

'You know me so well, Phyllis. But you weren't the only one wondering how he and his bride would share their time between London and Somerset.

His lordship's parents are both hale and hearty, with no desire to give up the duties involved in running the estate.'

'Go on.'

'A decision has been made.'

'Do get on with it, Norman!'

'Sorry. His lordship tells me that a house is to be built upon his father's land. Once all is ready, the young couple can reside there, as and when necessary. He intends to keep the London property as his base, but Miss Annabel in particular will become involved with a scheme both of them are keen on and with which Mr Crawford will be involved.'

'Not flying?'

Norman chuckled. 'I wouldn't put it past them, but this is horse breeding — in a small way, and as a sideline to the Crawford racing business. It will link the two families, and his lordship knows Annabel's father would miss her help.'

'She's not the sort to sit around at tea parties gossiping about high society.'

Phyllis grinned. 'Especially now she's marrying into it.'

'I haven't quite finished, my dear. Once the new house is complete, you and I will be spending time in Somerset as well as London. That's the plan, but I need to be sure you approve. It will be a challenge, but it means you'll still see something of Emmie.' He held his breath, hoping that would clinch the deal. Phyllis was the missing piece in his jigsaw.

'Norman Bassett, it feels like Christmas all over again. Of course I approve.'

He jumped up as someone tapped before pushing the door open. Annabel smiled at them both. Lawrence appeared behind her. Norman reckoned they both looked as if they'd flown to the stars and back.

'All in order, Mr Bassett?'

'Indeed, my lord.'

'So I'll still have you around to keep me on the straight and narrow?' Lawrence winked at Mrs Petts.

'Indeed you will, sir.'

We do hope that you have enjoyed reading this large print book.

Did you know that all of our titles are available for purchase?

We publish a wide range of high quality large print books including:
Romances, Mysteries, Classics General Fiction Non Fiction and Westerns

Special interest titles available in large print are:
The Little Oxford Dictionary Music Book, Song Book Hymn Book, Service Book

Also available from us courtesy of Oxford University Press:
Young Readers' Dictionary (large print edition) Young Readers' Thesaurus (large print edition)

For further information or a free brochure, please contact us at:
Ulverscroft Large Print Books Ltd., The Green, Bradgate Road, Anstey, Leicester, LE7 7FU, England. Tel: (00 44) **0116 236 4325 Fax:** (00 44) **0116 234 0205**

ENDLESS LOVE

Angela Britnell

Twenty years ago Gemma Sommerby
and Jack Watson shared a summer
romance, but after he left Cornwall
she never heard from him again. And
now, large as life and twice as handsome, he's back . . . Gemma can't
afford to open her heart to him
and risk being hurt again — and
Jack is just as disconcerted to find
she affects him as much as ever. Why
did it really go wrong between them
all those years ago? And could they
still have a future together?

THE EMERALD

Fay Cunningham

Cassandra Moon knows her mother Dora has a special talent — but will it be enough to protect the eccentric older lady when she is abducted in the depths of winter? Once again, Cass finds herself teaming up with DI Noel Raven, whom she argues with and is attracted to in equal measures. But the only way she and Noel can save Dora is to accept the bond of love that joins them together, so they can harness the power of the emerald ring and bring down the evil Constantine . . .

TROPICAL MADNESS

Nora Fountain

Paediatrician Serena Blake's idea of adventure is applying for a new hospital job in Dorset. Then her brother introduces her to the ruggedly handsome journalist and adventurer Jake Andrews, and she finds herself agreeing to accompany him to the African jungle in order to help sick and injured children. Soon the pair find themselves in the middle of an impending coup. And to make matters worse, Serena discovers that she's falling in love with Jake, though she's sure he will forget about her once — and *if* — they get back home . . .

HANDLE WITH CARE

Anne Hewland

Why is Leo Dryden so reluctant to explain to his daughter Jess the mystery surrounding her mother's death? Who is the charismatic Lucas, suddenly arriving with dramatic news? When Leo is rushed into hospital, Jess is left to face unforeseen dangers. Is the helpful Oliver all he seems? And then there is Sam, arriving alone in Leeds on a quest to find her beloved boyfriend Nat. But Lucas is involved with her too . . .

THE PRICE OF FOLLY

Denise Robins

All because of twenty-four hours in Paris, and an innocent mistake . . . Rich, handsome, sophisticated Alan Rivers sweeps Paula off her feet. His charming declarations of love and his fervent promises of marriage throw her into a sweet delirium of unreasoning bliss. But when she realises Alan's affections are as false as his promises, and her own feelings are mere infatuation, she soon comes to her senses. Can she free herself from the schemes of the vengeful Alan, and salvage a future with a man who really matters?